R.GOSCINNY– A.UDERZO

Asterix

ADVENTURE GAMES
ASTERIX TO THE RESCUE

Illustrated by Uderzo

HODDER AND STOUGHTON
LONDON SYDNEY AUCKLAND TORONTO

British Library Cataloguing in Publication Data

Asterix to the rescue – (Asterix adventure games)
   1. Games – Juvenile literature
   2. Adventure and adventures –
   Juvenile literature
   I. Title   II. Series
   793'.9   GV1203

   ISBN 0-340-38196-5

Published by Hodder and Stoughton Children's Books,
a division of Hodder and Stoughton Ltd,
Mill Road, Dunton Green, Sevenoaks, Kent TN13 2YJ

Photoset by Rowland Phototypesetting Ltd,
Bury St Edmunds, Suffolk

Printed in Great Britain by
Hazell Watson & Viney Limited,
Member of the BPCC Group,
Aylesbury, Bucks

You'll doubtless already be acquainted with Asterix's many adventures and his numerous confrontations with the mighty Roman army. Time and time again, this cunning little Gaul has put their Roman noses out of joint!

But Asterix and his overgrown friend, Obelix, now face perhaps their most challenging task of all . . . and that is why they have called upon YOU to take charge. Using various cards for assistance, YOU have to guide them through the many adventures and dangers that will accompany this mission.

You will not necessarily help them to the end of their mission on your first attempt. It may well take several goes. Keep trying, though, and they will eventually be successful.

Once they *have* successfully completed the mission, however, you can still take them on it again. For, there are many different routes they can follow – and each route involves different hazards and incidents.

So, the game can be played over and over again . . . as many times as you like!

HOW TO PLAY

To assist Asterix on his mission, you must guide him through a series of adventures in the book. You do this by starting at PARAGRAPH ONE and then following the instructions to other paragraphs.

Many of the paragraphs will present you with some sort of problem. It might be which password Asterix and Obelix are to use or how they are to find their way to the next town. You do not have to work out the answer for *every one* of the problems to guide them to the end of their mission . . . but the more you have success with, the more chance they'll have.

To help you deal with the problems, there are several useful items Asterix and Obelix can take on their mission – a map, a bag of coins (for bribes and to obtain information), a password scroll and a translator (for conversing with people of a different tongue). They can start with only *one* of these ITEMS but they will often gain others during the course of their mission.

The ITEM chosen for the two Gauls to start with (and any ITEMS they gain later) are to be kept, during the game, in the 'waist-slit' of the OBELIX CARD. This will tell you exactly which ITEMS you and they have for assistance at any one time (so, as soon as one of these ITEMS has helped in the answering of a problem, always remember to return it to the OBELIX CARD). Any ITEMS not contained in OBELIX's 'waist-slit' **are not to be used or consulted** – and therefore should be kept out of play.

A mission such as this one is bound to involve Asterix in many a skirmish with the Roman army. For this reason, he will be taking some gourds of magic potion with which to fortify himself. These MAGIC POTION CARDS are to be kept in the slit of the ASTERIX CARD.

Every time Asterix drinks a gourd of magic potion during the mission, you must remove one of the MAGIC POTION CARDS from the ASTERIX CARD. When there are no MAGIC POTION CARDS left in his 'waist-slit', it means he has run out of magic potion and he will not be strong enough to continue with the mission. He must therefore return to his village and you will have to start the game again from the beginning.

PREPARING FOR THE MISSION

The year is 50 BC. Gaul is entirely occupied by the Romans. Well, not entirely . . . Asterix's little village in the north-west corner still manages to hold out against the invaders. The secret of their success – apart from their great character and courage – lies in the magic potions brewed by an ancient Druid, Getafix. These bestow on the drinker a superhuman strength which make him the match for a whole garrison of Romans.

But disaster has hit the village! While out searching for the ingredients for his magic potion, Getafix is seized by a gang of Roman kidnappers. It is later learnt that he has been taken to Rome so that Caesar can find out the secret of the magic potion for himself. Should Getafix be forced to reveal it, that would immediately be the end of the village's brave resistance!

Distraught, the chief of the village instructs Asterix and his friend Obelix – who also insists on taking his pet dog, Dogmatix – to travel to Rome to try and rescue the Druid. He realises that finding their way across Europe won't be at all easy, however, and so offers them a collection of useful items to help. There is a map to show the main towns, a bag of coins to be used as bribes, a translator to work out what non-Gauls are saying, and a scroll of all the passwords they might require. Obelix says he will only be able to take one of these, however, for, although he is certainly big enough to carry all four, he wants to be as unladen as possible for fighting all those lovely Romans! Besides, they might be able to pick up the rest of the items on the way.

What the chief of the village *insists* that the two travellers take with them, though, is some gourds of magic potion. Although the potion is not necessary for one as strong as Obelix (who fell into a cauldron of the potion as a baby and now has to be kept away from it!), it is absolutely essential for Asterix. Fortunately, Getafix had the good sense to keep several gourds of the special liquid in reserve . . .

Your first task, then, is to decide which ITEM the two Gauls are to take on their journey. Which of the four do you think would be the most useful – a map, a password scroll, a translator or bag of coins? Insert the ITEM you have chosen into the slit of the OBELIX

CARD and keep the remaining three ITEMS out of play until such time as you are told to pick them up.

Now to give Asterix his magic potions. The *number* of magic potions you give him depends entirely on how difficult you would like the mission to be. If you would like a fairly easy mission, then put all three MAGIC POTION CARDS into the slit of the ASTERIX CARD. If you would like a harder mission, put only two, or even one, MAGIC POTION CARDS into the slit. Don't forget to remove a MAGIC POTION CARD every time you are instructed to do so . . . and, remember, when there are none left, the mission has to stop and you must start it again from the beginning.

NB. The game can be played either as a **luck** game or a **skill** game. A **luck** game entails letting the special Asterix DICE determine the course you take. A **skill** game entails using your memory and experience to determine your course. This skill will increase the more times you play. If you decide on the **skill** game, whenever you come across a 'throw the special DICE' instruction, you simply use your own judgment to determine between the options instead.

You are now ready to set off on the mission. May the Gods be with you!

The villagers all came out to wave goodbye as Asterix and Obelix started on their long journey. 'Best of luck,' the chief of the village, Vitalstatistix, shouted after them, 'and remember, the freedom of everyone here depends upon you!' The small fortification was soon no more than a tiny speck behind them and Obelix gave a deep sigh, thinking that it would be several weeks before he saw it again. But then he thought of all the Roman garrisons ahead of them and began to rub his hands in anticipation. Our Gaulish friends had walked quite a way further when the road they were on suddenly divided three ways. 'I reckon *this* must be the branch we want,' said Asterix, pointing to the one that went to the right. Obelix didn't agree, though, preferring the one in the middle . . . and nor did Dogmatix, wagging his tail at the one on the left! 'Well, we can't all go different ways,' said Asterix in exasperation. 'I know all roads are meant to lead to Rome but this is ridiculous!' He therefore insisted that they come to some sort of agreement.

Throw the special DICE to decide whose choice they should follow.

If you throw ASTERIX	go to 162
If you throw OBELIX	go to 124
If you throw DOGMATIX	go to 151

'Look, *there's* somewhere!' exclaimed Obelix, suddenly pointing out a sign that read 'The Frog and Snail' halfway down the next street. Rubbing his huge tummy, he hurriedly led the way towards it. After they had ordered their favourite snack of barbecued boar-ribs, they went to sit near to some Romans eating there, intending to eavesdrop on their conversation. 'Maybe they'll mention something about Getafix,' Asterix whispered behind his hand as they moved as near as they dared. But then he realised there was a problem. The Romans were speaking in their native Latin and the only way they'd be able to understand them was with a translator.

Does OBELIX have a TRANSLATOR with him? If so, use it to find out what the Romans were saying by translating the instruction in the speech-balloon below. If he doesn't have one, go to 47 instead.

SUT LIM OPPI TRO

Obelix told the peasant that he didn't have any coins on him, however. 'Then you won't get my information,' the peasant said, hurriedly leaving by the door. Asterix had only taken a couple more sips of his drink when he started to feel rather peculiar. He felt as if all his strength had gone and it was as much as he could do to hold up his tankard. 'That peasant must have slipped something into my beer to weaken me,' he said. 'I'd better take a magic potion to reverse the effect.' Fortunately, he was soon back to his old self again, telling his friend that he had never known such an unpleasant peasant!

*Remove a **MAGIC POTION CARD** from **ASTERIX'S WAIST-SLIT**. Now go to 66.*

4

'Ah, this is a much nicer way to travel,' exclaimed Asterix, lying back on the hay as the cart trundled along the road. 'It's far better than on foot!' Obelix replied that they were 'on foot', though – the feet of the ox that was pulling the cart! 'Well, what I meant was that it was far better than walking,' said Asterix, becoming a little irritated. Obelix told him that the ox *was* walking, though – if it was running, they would have been moving a lot faster! *Go to 154.*

5

The first to cross the river was Dogmatix – doing, of course, the dog paddle! Next to swim to the other side was Asterix and then Obelix (although he displaced so much water with his frantic arm strokes that it was almost a case of walking across!). After drying out on the bank, the three travellers took the road again, eventually arriving at a barrier with a little wooden kiosk at the side. The Roman inside the kiosk said that there was a toll for the next part of the road and they would have to pay two coins to pass.

Does OBELIX have a COINBAG with him? If so, 'count out' the two coins by rotating the disc – then turn to the number that appears on the other side. If he doesn't have one, go to 101 instead.

6

'I'm afraid *WOLF* is wrong,' the Romans told them haughtily. 'You'll just have to find another way round the gorge!' But just as the rope-car was about to leave, the Gauls quickly jumped on, waving the Romans a cheeky goodbye. They were about halfway across the gorge, however, when the hook tying the top of the little wooden cabin to the rope sounded as if it was about to snap. 'I'd better do something,' said Asterix urgently, 'or we're going to plunge right into the valley!' So he quickly drank one of his magic potions and then climbed on to the roof, where – with one hand gripping the rope and the other the cabin – he safely supported them to the other side. 'Honestly, Roman engineering!' he exclaimed as he rubbed his sore palms.

Remove a MAGIC POTION CARD from ASTERIX'S WAIST-SLIT. Now go to 84.

The Narbo galley had sailed quite a way along the coast when Asterix suddenly realised that a lot of the crew were Hispanic. 'And you know what that means?' he asked his friend with concern. 'We're probably heading for Hispania – the wrong direction!' They were just wondering how they were going to get back when their galley was attacked by a gang of pirates. The Gauls were clapped in irons by the cut-throats and locked below deck – but they didn't mind for the moment because the pirate ship was heading back towards Italia! As soon as the ship had reached Italian waters, however, Asterix drank one of his magic potions and he and his friend knocked all the pirates out before swimming for the shore. 'Nice of them to put us in the right direction again!' Obelix chuckled as they dried out on the Italian sand.

Remove a MAGIC POTION CARD from ASTERIX'S WAIST-SLIT. Now go to 220. (Remember: when there are no magic potion cards left in Asterix's waist-slit their mission has to stop, and you must start the game again.)

Suddenly spotting the baths from all the steam coming out of the building, Obelix led the way up the stairs. Asterix undressed right down to his birthday suit, as he saw others doing, but Obelix was a little shy, insisting on keeping his ribbons in his hair! The three of them were just having a nice soak in the heated water when a Roman attendant started shouting something across the baths at them. 'You don't have a translator amongst your clothes by any chance?' Asterix asked his friend with concern.

If OBELIX does have a TRANSLATOR, use it to find out what the attendant was saying by translating the content of his speech-balloon below. If he doesn't, go to 178 instead.

9

They had walked quite a few miles along the road to Aregenua when they spotted a small band of Roman soldiers coming the other way. The Gauls quickly jumped into a nearby hedge, watching them pass. 'Look, they've all got big grins on their faces,' Asterix whispered. 'That suggests they're returning to Rome!' It also suggested, of course, that the three travellers had been going in the wrong direction and so they decided the best thing to do was to follow in the Romans' footsteps. 'Not too close, though,' Asterix warned his big friend. 'We don't want to spoil their leave!' *Go to 117.*

'So you *are* Gaulish spies, then!' the Romans' leader yelled at them when *SHIELD* had obviously proved wrong. Refusing to let them have a second guess, he immediately ordered his men to take them away. 'Would you mind waiting a couple of seconds?' Asterix asked politely and, while they obliged, he quickly drank one of his magic potions. 'That's better!' he exclaimed . . . and immediately knocked three of the Romans out in one blow! Soon there was only the leader left standing, but a quick clonk under the chin finished him off too. 'Yes, you *can* have a second guess,' the dazed captain whined after them as the Gauls wandered off into the town. 'Three guesses, four guesses . . . any number you want!'

Remove a MAGIC POTION CARD from ASTERIX'S WAIST-SLIT. Now go to 149.

'. . . So the cobbler was right – you *are* spies!' the captain said, after he had told them that their guess at *HELMET* was wrong. Asterix quickly drank one of his magic potions and then informed the cobbler that they would just be stepping outside for a minute. 'Perhaps you could have my shoes ready for when I come back in?' he added politely. The cobbler just laughed at this but, sure enough, a minute (and twenty knocked-out Romans) later the barely ruffled Gauls re-entered the shop. 'I'll be as quick as I can,' the terrified cobbler told them . . . and it was the fastest pair of shoes he ever made!

Remove a MAGIC POTION CARD from ASTERIX'S WAIST-SLIT. Now go to 79.

Since the Gauls didn't have any money with them, the guards said they would have to leave – or be thrown to the lions themselves! 'I'm afraid we don't believe in cruelty to animals . . .' Obelix retorted, while his little friend drank one of his magic potions. When the guards were all sprawled unconscious down the steps, the Gauls continued on their way. '. . . Only cruelty to Romans,' Obelix added with a chuckle as they headed for the dungeons.

Remove a MAGIC POTION CARD from ASTERIX'S WAIST-SLIT. Now go to 87. (Remember: when there are no magic potion cards left in Asterix's waist-slit their mission has to stop, and you must start the game again.)

13

Not having a translator, the Gauls decided just to hope for the best and continue down the steps. 'Hurry up, prisoner!' Asterix ordered his friend with a gentle prod in the back, still keeping up the pretence. But the Romans obviously *hadn't* been taken in by this little act because they suddenly drew out their swords! Asterix quickly drank one of his magic potions in reply and then helped Obelix start knocking them down the steps. When the soldiers were all finally out of the way, the Gauls continued towards the dungeons. 'Can we play that game again now?' Obelix asked eagerly, raising his hands as if he was still Asterix's prisoner!

Remove a MAGIC POTION CARD from ASTERIX'S WAIST-SLIT. Now go to 107. (Remember: when there are no magic potion cards left in Asterix's waist-slit their mission is over, and you must start the game again.)

14

Our Gaulish friends were soon taking to the road again, knowing that they couldn't delay anywhere for too long. 'It's beginning to get dark,' said Asterix, after they had passed a good ten milestones or so, 'we'd better look for a suitable place to sleep in the bushes.' They at last found somewhere but dozing off proved more difficult than they expected. The trouble was that they were normally used to being sent to sleep by the singing of Cacofonix, their bard. It wasn't that his voice was tuneful – it was just that sleep was the only way to block it out! So they decided just to pretend Cacofonix was singing, imagining his awful wail. It seemed to do the trick, their eyelids gradually becoming heavier . . .

Throw the special DICE to decide who is to drop off first.

If you throw ASTERIX   go to 225
If you throw OBELIX   go to 250
If you throw DOGMATIX   go to 279

Obelix and Dogmatix now returned to the business of choosing their drinks. Obelix eventually decided on a barrel of beer and Dogmatix gave a couple of woofs to indicate that he would like some goat's milk. 'I'm afraid you might be a bit unlucky with the goat's milk,' the innkeeper apologised when Obelix had translated Dogmatix's order for him, 'the goat standing on the bar has just been emptied.' Fortunately, however, he found that he had another one down in the cellar and so Dogmatix was to get his choice after all!
Go to 66.

16

Their road went on and on but the two Gauls at last came to the town of Vellaunodunum. After having spent the previous night in the open, they all agreed that they would like a nice bed this time and so they decided to stop over until the morning. The Roman at the gates seemed to have other ideas. 'You can only enter if you know the town password,' he said, blocking their way with his sword, 'and if you give the wrong password, you must be spies and so you will be taken to the circus at Rome!'

Does OBELIX have a PASSWORD SCROLL with him? If so, use it to find out what the correct password is by placing exactly

over the scroll shape below – then follow the appropriate
instruction. If he doesn't have one, you'll have to guess which
instruction to follow.

If you think it's SWORD	go to 184
If you think it's JAVELIN	go to 118
If you think it's DAGGER	go to 89

17

It was immediately obvious that *JAVELIN* was wrong because the
waiter summoned two huge bouncers – and a Great Dane for
Dogmatix! – from the back. Normally, of course, Asterix and

Obelix would have relished this challenge but they were reluctant to use their strength against other Gauls (however big they were!). So they meekly allowed themselves to be thrown out on to the street. 'What a pity,' said Obelix as he brushed himself down, 'that Boar à la King sounded rather tasty!' *Go to 67.*

18

The Romans told them that *NEPTUNE* was incorrect, however, and that they should turn away because they were holding everyone up. 'Yes, hurry and move out of the way,' said a small, fussing peasant's wife behind them. 'We're on holiday and we don't want to spend it all in this queue!' Asterix asked her to wait just a few seconds longer, though, while he drank one of his magic potions. And it was only a few seconds after *that* that all the Romans were lying on the ground! 'The queue seems to be moving very nicely now,' remarked Obelix as they and everyone else filed through the empty checkpoint. 'I think it was a bit unfair of those Romans to accuse us of holding it up!'

Remove a MAGIC POTION CARD from ASTERIX'S WAIST-SLIT. Now go to 91.

Not having a translator with them, the Gauls could do nothing but scratch their heads! This seemed to make the pirates even more angry than they were already and they drew out their cutlasses, ready to cut them down. 'I think I'd better have one of my magic potions!' Asterix remarked casually, and Obelix held the pirates off for a moment so the little Gaul could savour every last drop. Then it was a quick clonk . . . thud . . . whack . . . and the pirates were all tossed into the water below! 'I've just realised what they might have been trying to tell us . . .' Obelix said slowly as he wiped his hands, '. . . I think they wanted us to walk the plank!'

Remove a MAGIC POTION CARD from ASTERIX'S WAIST-SLIT. Now go to 167.

After a long hard journey across the Helvetian mountains, the Gauls finally arrived at a large barrier guarded by Romans. 'It looks like a frontier post,' Asterix remarked to his friend. 'We must be leaving Helvetia and crossing into Italia!' When they walked right up to the barrier, however, the Romans said that they could only pass if they knew the correct password.

Does OBELIX carry a PASSWORD SCROLL with him? If so, use it to find out the correct password by placing exactly over the

scroll shape below – then go to the appropriate number. If he doesn't, you'll have to guess which number to go to.

```
A S    K N    PP    R
 H A   T K E J   D B
   U     GU P     I H
   L    S 8 OP    T H L
   A C D L   B  A F TW
   N T  EH   U G I E
   L R   N T  U V Y
   P 7 U 1  6     S & T
    R S &   U 6   S N
   E GQ O S N L      M
    2   N L 0K E   E
```

If you think it's AUGUSTUS	go to 196
If you think it's JULIUS	go to 129
If you think it's TIBERIUS	go to 228

21

Early next morning, the Gauls were on the road again. As lunch-time approached, they arrived at the large town of Dertona and they decided to stop there for a while. 'Isn't it big!' Obelix exclaimed as they walked amongst all the magnificent stone buildings. 'I bet the menhir business does very well here!' After a quick take-away lunch of boarburgers, Asterix suggested they search for one of the famous Roman baths they'd heard so much about so they could have a wash. 'Just look for a building with lots of clean Romans coming out!' he said as they wandered through the streets.

Throw the special DICE to decide who is to spot the baths first.

If you throw ASTERIX	go to 70
If you throw OBELIX	go to 8
If you throw DOGMATIX	go to 113

22

Since they didn't have a translator with them, the Gauls started to turn away from the hut. They had only gone a few steps, however, when the woman called them back again – and this time in their own tongue. 'I just wanted to make sure you weren't Romans in disguise,' she explained, 'so I spoke in Latin to see whether you would understand me. Since you didn't, you're quite welcome to come inside!' As they were entering the hut, though, there was a bit of a misfortune. Asterix tripped over the tip of his sword and burst one of his gourds of magic potion as he fell.

Remove a MAGIC POTION CARD from ASTERIX'S WAIST-SLIT. Now go to 203.

When the Gauls had come to the end of the Populonia road, it was only to find that it was totally the wrong direction for Rome. Fortunately, though, the town of Populonia was next to the sea and so they could take a galley there instead. Looking at a timetable, they saw that one was about to set sail for Rome in the next few seconds. 'It must be that one over there!' Asterix exclaimed, pointing to the end of the harbour, and they all made a dash for it as the gangplank was being pulled in. They just managed to leap aboard in time but, as he jumped, Asterix dropped one of his gourds of magic potion into the sea below!

Remove a *MAGIC POTION CARD* from *ASTERIX'S WAIST-SLIT. Now go to 45.* (Remember: when there are no magic potion cards left in Asterix's waist-slit their mission has to stop, and you must start the game again.)

24

The Romans replied that *ARMOUR* was correct, letting them pass. But, just as the Gauls were thinking that they had got away with it, one of the Romans called after them. 'Hang on a minute,' he ordered suspiciously. 'If you're doctors, why have you got swords with you?' Asterix had another quick think . . . 'Oh, that's how we test the victim's heart,' he replied casually. 'We pretend we're about to stab them with the sword – and, if their heart can stand up to that shock, then it can probably stand up to the lions too.' Much to the little Gaul's surprise, the Romans believed him and let them continue towards the dungeons! ***Go to 107.***

'*I've* picked the shortest blade of grass!' Obelix announced excitedly and he went straight up to the sentry at the gates. 'Hello,' he said, 'we're sworn enemies of Rome and we should like to enter the town.' Unable to believe his ears, Asterix immediately dragged him back. 'What sort of distraction is that?' he asked furiously, but Obelix said he'd rather lost interest in the distraction idea, preferring a nice fight! Asterix said that they needed to preserve their energy for the journey, though, and suggested they move on to the next town before the alarm was raised. Still a little annoyed with him, he asked Obelix if he had a map so they could find out which town was the nearest.

If OBELIX does have a MAP, use it to work out which of the three towns below is closest to Alauna – then follow the instruction. If he doesn't have one, you'll have to guess which instruction to follow.

If you think it's AREGENUA   go to 139
If you think it's NOVIODUNUM   go to 171
If you think it's ARAINES   go to 270

'Here you are, my good lady,' said Asterix politely as he passed the eighteen coins to the woman, doffing his helmet at the same time. But Obelix suddenly grabbed the coins back, insisting that they wait a minute. 'First, I want to know what breakfast is!' he demanded. The landlady had a think for a moment. 'Well, let me see now,' she said. 'Tomorrow it's either croissants, or a cooked breakfast, or Danish boar and eggs.' At this, Obelix's face turned into a big, stupid grin and the poor woman was half-suffocated as he hugged her. *Go to 203.*

They had been waiting for the cart for Lutetia to start when one of the other passengers told them that the cart for Vellaunodunum went more in the direction they wanted. So they quickly jumped off, just catching the Vellaunodunum one in time. As the cart trundled through the countryside, however, it suddenly hit a large rock and Asterix was thrown off on to the road. Fortunately, his helmet protected him from a nasty bruise but his sword pierced one of his gourds of magic potion as he landed. 'I wish these cart-drivers would look where they're going!' he remarked angrily as he climbed back on again.

Remove a MAGIC POTION CARD from ASTERIX'S

WAIST-SLIT. *Now go to 154.* (Remember: when there are no magic potion cards left in Asterix's waist-slit their mission has to stop, and you must start the game again from the beginning.)

28

'Yelp, yelp, yelp!' Dogmatix suddenly started barking, his paw pointing to some hazy mountain tops in the distance. Obelix patted his little dog on the head for being the first to spot them – although he told him they were called **Alps**, not **Yelps**! They had only walked a few miles further when they reached a barrier across the road, guarded by Roman soldiers. 'I wonder what that's for?' said Asterix but, when he asked one of the soldiers, the reply came in Latin. 'I don't suppose you have a translator on you?' he enquired, turning to Obelix.

If OBELIX does have one, use it to find out what the Roman was saying by translating the content of his speech-balloon below. If he doesn't, go to 211 instead.

The road to Cambodunum took the Gauls through a large, black forest and Obelix suggested they go hunting for some of those tiny wild boar they had just eaten. 'I know you need quite a lot to make a decent snack,' he said, 'but they were really quite delicious!' Asterix tried to explain that they weren't really boar at all . . . but Obelix had already excitedly disappeared into the trees with his dog. 'I'm afraid Dogmatix couldn't sniff any,' Obelix told him disappointedly after half an hour or so. 'He *did* manage to find this password scroll, however!'

If OBELIX doesn't already carry it, put the PASSWORD SCROLL into his WAIST-SLIT. Now go to 157.

They hadn't gone far along the Dertona road when they were told by an innkeeper that they were only two miles from the Italian frontier. 'In some ways I'll be sad to leave Helvetia,' said Asterix as he drank a goblet of delicious mountain goat's milk. 'But in some ways I won't!' he added as a deafening yodelling sound from the valley started to vibrate their table. The frontier was heavily guarded by a decury of Romans (a unit of ten) and so Obelix started to make a massive snowball, rolling it round and round until it was the size of a house. Then he hurled it at the soldiers, knocking every single one of them out. 'I've always enjoyed a bit of ten-pin bowling!' Obelix chuckled as the Gauls crossed into Italia. ***Go to 220.***

31

The word *AUGUSTUS* had hardly left Obelix's lips when the Roman drew his sword. 'No, that's wrong,' he barked, 'the rebels must be you two!' Obelix was a little offended that he hadn't counted Dogmatix as a rebel as well but he didn't want to make a big fuss about it . . . so he only swung each Roman *three* times around his head instead of four! As they all slid unconscious to the floor, Asterix gave the innkeeper one of his gourds of magic potion. 'Put a few drops of that into every drink you serve,' he told him with a wink, 'and your customers need never have to worry about the Romans again!'

Remove a *MAGIC POTION CARD* from *ASTERIX'S WAIST-SLIT*. Now go to 66.

32

They hadn't walked far along the road to Vellaunodunum when they caught up with a travelling merchant trying to lead his stubborn horse. 'He just doesn't seem to have any horsepower any more,' the merchant told them miserably as he gave it another tug, '– how on earth am I going to get all my wares to the market?' Since the merchant's wares were obviously wearing the horse down, Obelix offered to carry it some of the way. 'Don't worry,' he reassured the surprised merchant as he lifted both horse and wares on to his broad back, 'they're much lighter than the menhirs I usually carry!' The merchant was so grateful for their assistance that he offered the Gauls a translator.

If OBELIX doesn't already carry it, put the TRANSLATOR into his WAIST-SLIT. Now go to 16.

33

Obelix didn't have a translator, however, and so there seemed no other way but to shut the sentry up by force. Obelix was about to grab hold of his scrawny neck but Asterix told him to stand aside while he dealt with him. 'Since it was your big mouth that was responsible for this,' he said, 'you can jolly well watch someone else have the pleasure!' The sentry was soon left in a knotted heap on the ground but the fight hadn't all gone Asterix's way. One of his gourds of magic potion had been pierced by the sentry's pike and now dripped on to his feet!

*Remove a **MAGIC POTION CARD** from **ASTERIX'S WAIST-SLIT**. Now go to 81.*

34

Once inside the palace, the Gauls crept past room after room, hoping to overhear something at one of the doors. At last they did – and it was coming from the mouth of Caesar himself! He seemed to be addressing one of his advisers and, although he was speaking in Latin, the Gauls could catch the name 'Getafix' every so often! Listening harder, they also caught the words 'Colosseum' and '*carcer septem*'. 'It sounds like he's being kept in the dungeons just below the Colosseum,' Asterix whispered to his friend, 'and it's cell number seven!' *Go to 150.*

35

Since they couldn't make head or tail of what the Roman was saying, Obelix dropped him on his head! 'We'll just have to rely on our instincts to find the road again,' said Asterix, beginning to lead the

way through the trees. Fortunately, their instincts proved reliable
and they were soon following the road towards a town called
Alauna. Obelix wondered whether they would be able to buy some
wild boar there but Asterix told him to talk about something else for
a while – he was beginning to be a bit of a bore himself! **Go to 55.**

36

When he had taken the seven coins from Obelix, the old man led
them from one street to another, telling them all about himself as he
went. He listed all the battles he had fought in and said how life was
much harder when he was a lad without any of these modern con-
veniences. 'But they were good old days!' he kept mumbling
through his long beard. Rather relieved, the Gauls at last found
themselves at their destination. Just as they were about to enter the
inn, though, the old man produced a map of the Roman Empire
from his grubby clothes. He said since they had been so generous to
him they could have it, free, for their travels.

**If OBELIX doesn't already carry it, put the MAP into his
WAIST-SLIT. Now go to 108.**

37

'They want us to go with them to become galley-slaves,' said Obelix,
quickly reading through his translator as the Romans spoke.
Suddenly, though, the Romans all ran off as fast as their legs could

carry them. 'I wonder why they changed their minds,' said Obelix, scratching his head, but then Asterix pointed out that it was probably because he had torn his chains apart. 'Oh yes, so I have,' Obelix replied, only just noticing. 'I must have done it when I reached for the translator!' They were just about to continue on their journey when Dogmatix spotted a coinbag in the grass. It must have dropped from one of the Romans' pockets in his panic!

If OBELIX doesn't already carry it, put the COINBAG into his WAIST-SLIT. Now go to 16.

38

Since Obelix didn't have a map, they decided to chance the road for Lutetia. They had been walking for quite a way when Asterix suddenly noticed something peculiar about Dogmatix. He was balancing a large rock, two or three times his size, on his nose! Then he realised what had happened. One of his gourds of magic potion was leaking and Dogmatix had been lapping the drops up behind him!

Remove a MAGIC POTION CARD from ASTERIX'S WAIST-SLIT. Now go to 154. (Remember: when there are no magic potion cards left in Asterix's waist-slit their mission has to stop, and you must start again from the beginning.)

The Gauls now left Alesia, starting their journey again. The land about them gradually rose higher and higher, and the air seemed to become much fresher. 'We should soon be able to see the Alps!' said Asterix, searching the horizon for their snowy peaks. His two companions began to look for them as well, each hoping that they would spot them first.

Throw the special DICE to decide which one it will be.

If you throw ASTERIX   go to 74
If you throw OBELIX   go to 119
If you throw DOGMATIX   go to 28

When Asterix and Obelix had joined their little dog on the galley, they all went to look for a good place to sunbathe while the crew started to cast off. 'Ah, this is the life!' Asterix exclaimed as they stretched out on the deck. 'Yes, a couple of nice roast boar each,' his greedy friend added, 'and it would be perfect bliss!' They hadn't sailed far up the coastline, however, when a pirate ship appeared in the distance. Soon the pirates were starting to board their galley. Waving cutlasses at them, they forced both the Gauls and all the crew members into a corner, giving them some sort of order. It was in a strange language, however, and it would need a translator to find out what they were after.

Does OBELIX have a TRANSLATOR with him? If so, use it to work out what the pirates wanted by translating the content of the speech-balloon below. If he doesn't, go to 19 instead.

SUT LIM OPPI TIMA

41

Not only did the Roman let them pass for their two coins but he also offered them a free translator. He said that they would soon be reaching the country of Germania and the language of the people there was very different. 'Well, it's nice to see that *some* Romans are friendly,' Asterix remarked as they walked through the barrier. Obelix rather objected to friendly Romans, though – it gave him no excuse for hitting them!

If OBELIX doesn't already carry it, put the TRANSLATOR into his WAIST-SLIT. Now go to 128.

'They're telling us that we're at the border with Italia,' Obelix said as he glanced up and down his translator, '. . . and they want to know why we want to cross.' Asterix tried to think of a good answer for a moment. 'I know,' he suddenly exclaimed, telling Obelix to translate back for him. 'Say that we want to take part in the circus at Rome!' The Romans could barely hide their sniggering, not only letting them pass but even offering them a map so they would know how to get there. 'I rather got the impression that they thought we were a bit stupid!' Obelix remarked as they left Noricum behind.

If OBELIX doesn't already carry it, put the MAP into his WAIST-SLIT. Now go to 220.

Since he was leader on this mission, the other two let Asterix go through the turnstile first. They then followed him up a number of stone steps, eventually finding themselves in the middle of a vast stadium! 'I've suddenly realised what this is,' Asterix said as they sat down at the end of a long bench. 'It's a place for circuses – where people are thrown to the lions!' Unfortunately, though, a Roman soldier sitting behind overheard him and, recognising his language as Gaulish, immediately had them arrested as spies. Asterix said that they were tourists, however, and were just spending a holiday there. 'In that case, your travel agent should have told you the password for the city,' the Roman replied. 'If you can't tell me what it is, you won't be watching the circus but *appearing* in it!'

Does OBELIX have a PASSWORD SCROLL with him? If so, use it to find out the correct password by placing exactly over the scroll shape below – then follow the appropriate instruction. If he doesn't have one you'll have to guess which instruction to follow.

If you think it's LION   go to 254
If you think it's WOLF   go to 188
If you think it's EAGLE   go to 235

'He's telling us that they're the bodyguard for the consul's son,' Obelix said, becoming more and more angry-looking as he translated. 'And, apparently, the little brat would like to take Dogmatix home for a pet!' Asterix thought it only fair to let Obelix deal with this outrage himself, and so he calmly examined the sandals again while his friend gave the Romans a piece of his mind; not to mention a piece of his fist! 'You know, prices are so expensive these days,' Asterix remarked casually when Obelix was at last finished, having hurled the Romans right across the square! *Go to 79.*

Mid-afternoon of the following day, the Gauls at last reached Rome. Their long journey was finally over! 'What a magnificent city!' Asterix exclaimed in awe as they looked round at all the beautiful buildings. They couldn't stand there appreciating it for long, though, because there was work to be done. 'I suggest we search out Caesar's palace first,' Asterix said, 'and then try and sneak in to see if we can find out exactly where Getafix is being kept prisoner.' They soon found the palace – a magnificent, heavily-guarded building on a hill – and they quickly discussed who was going to go up to the gates first.

Throw the special DICE to decide.

If you throw ASTERIX	go to 223
If you throw OBELIX	go to 180
If you throw DOGMATIX	go to 207

When the Gauls had passed the twelve coins through the bars, the guard started to unlock the cell door so he could come and direct them. 'As soon as he steps out,' Asterix whispered to Obelix, 'bash him over the head!' Obelix gladly obliged, knocking the guard completely senseless, and then he and his two friends hurried into the cell. They all looked round for Getafix, suddenly spotting him in the corner . . . *Go to 158.*

Just as Obelix was telling Asterix that he didn't have a translator with him, there was a piercing scream from the Roman next to them. Dogmatix had bitten one of his bare toes, mistakenly thinking that it was a piece of boar rib that had fallen off someone's plate! When the howling Roman gave Dogmatix a kick, that was it! Obelix hurled him across the table and it was soon an almighty free-for-all as Asterix and all the other Romans joined in. 'I think we had better look for another place to eat,' Asterix wisely proposed as they finally stepped over the mass of swooning bodies. They at last found another inn, Asterix downing a gourd of magic potion before they entered. All that brawling had taken its toll!

Remove a MAGIC POTION CARD from ASTERIX'S WAIST-SLIT. Now go to 108.

48

When they had paid for their breakfast, they continued on their travels. 'I love wild mushrooms with my wild boar,' said Obelix, still licking his lips. Over the next mile or so, he quietly tried to think how you made mushrooms wild. With boar, it was easy – you just kept chasing them until they lost their temper. But you surely couldn't chase mushrooms? *Go to 16.*

49

When Obelix had paid him their nineteen-coin fare, the captain said he would be delighted to have them at his table for dinner. 'Will it be a boar?' Obelix asked hungrily but the captain said that would depend on the rest of the guests – sometimes they were boring, sometimes they weren't! He then told them at which ports the galley was to stop in Italia and offered them a translator to get the most out of their visit.

If OBELIX doesn't already carry it, put the TRANSLATOR into his WAIST-SLIT. Now go to 167.

50

They had been following the Vindonissa road for a couple of miles when they saw a signpost pointing to Italia. Unfortunately, though, it pointed in the direction they had just come and so they had to go all the way back again! 'Let's try the Bergomum road this time,' Asterix suggested when they were back at the three roads. *Go to 20.*

51

'*WOLF* is absolutely right!' the leader of the Romans exclaimed with some surprise. 'But, if you're from this area, how is it that you've never seen a pizza before?' Asterix calmly took another bite of the pizza to give himself time to think. 'Of course we've seen pizzas before,' he cunningly replied. 'It's just that we've never seen one with this particular topping. We always put wild mushrooms on ours!' Obelix decided to assist his friend in the lie. 'Yes, and a few wild boar . . .' he added enthusiastically but Asterix quickly apologised for him, pretending to the Romans that he was a bit simple. In fact, he sometimes wondered whether he really was! *Go to 21.*

52

The Gauls' long journey through Italia continued, the distance to Rome gradually decreasing. After another three hard days of walking, a milestone showed them that there were only a hundred miles to go! Asterix's shoes had worn so thin, however, that he insisted they stop off at the very next town to buy some more. That town was Narnia and they wandered around the dusty streets, looking for a cobbler's.

Throw the special DICE to decide who is to spot one first.

If you throw ASTERIX	go to 230
If you throw OBELIX	go to 276
If you throw DOGMATIX	go to 130

53

As soon as they had paid the galley-owner the ten coins, the three Gauls walked along the gangplank to the harbour. 'It will have to be a very quick breakfast I'm afraid,' Asterix told his hungry friend as they looked round for somewhere to eat. 'We can't afford to waste much time.' So it was only ten minutes between finding a little tavern and then leaving again. Asterix had had a croissant with myrtleberry jam, Dogmatix a few ox-scraps, and Obelix . . . four whole boar, seven chickens and a couple of vats of goat's milk. Well, Asterix had only said that it had to be a *quick* breakfast – he didn't say anything about its size! ***Go to 149.***

Fortunately, Obelix had just enough in his bag to pay the fifteen coins. 'Hang on a minute,' one of the guards said just as they were about to let them pass. 'This coin looks like a forgery!' Asterix put his hand to a magic potion in anticipation of trouble but, after a closer look at the coin, the guard decided it was the real thing after all. 'Those Romans are so distrustful!' Asterix remarked to his friend as they now continued towards the dungeons. ***Go to 87.***

55

The town of Alauna now appeared ahead, and they agreed that one of them should distract the sentry at the gate while the others sneaked past. Asterix suggested they draw straws for it but Obelix said it would be unfair on Dogmatix, since he would have difficulty holding the crayon. 'No, I mean pick straws for it, you bird-brain!' Asterix sighed and plucked three unequal lengths of grass to show Obelix what he meant. 'The one who picks the shortest is the one to do the distracting,' he explained.

Throw the special DICE to decide who it's to be.

If you throw ASTERIX	go to 192
If you throw OBELIX	go to 25
If you throw DOGMATIX	go to 242

'That sounds like an inn!' Asterix exclaimed, suddenly hearing happy singing from the end of the next street. Entering the inn, they started to ask round about Getafix but no one could give a coherent reply. 'Isn't it marvellous?' Asterix remarked with exasperation. 'The only time the people in this town are hospitable, everyone's too drunk to make any sense!' So they decided to leave Noviodunum and call in at the next town on the way to Rome. A signpost just outside the gates pointed to the neighbouring towns of Araines, Aregenua and Alauna; and Asterix asked his friend if he had a map so they could look up which was in the right direction.

Does OBELIX have a MAP on him? If so, use it to find out which of the three towns is on the way to Rome from Noviodunum – then follow the appropriate instruction. If he doesn't have one, you'll have to guess which instruction to follow.

If you think ARAINES	go to 255
If you think AREGENUA	go to 9
If you think ALAUNA	go to 152

As soon as Obelix had paid him the twenty coins, the innkeeper hid the two Gauls in a secret hole under the floor. He let Dogmatix sit by the fire, pretending that he was his own dog. After they had a good look round, the Romans were just about to go again when their leader noticed that there were three large plates of boar on the table. He demanded to know whose they were but the innkeeper said they were for his dog, who had a surprisingly large appetite for such a small animal. 'Well, you want to be careful, dog,' the Roman told Dogmatix as he left, 'or you'll end up looking like that fat Gaul, Obelix!' *Go to 143.*

58

Spurred on by the thought of roast boar, it was Obelix who reached the inn first. Asterix arrived soon after but, just as the two Gauls were about to enter the inn, they noticed that Dogmatix was missing. Looking all round, they suddenly spotted him in the distance – being taken away by a patrol of Romans! They immediately ran after the patrol, a furious Obelix demanding what they were doing with his dog. One of the Romans replied in Latin, and so they were going to need a translator!

Does OBELIX carry a TRANSLATOR with him? If so, use it to

find out what the Roman was saying by translating the content of the speech-balloon below. If not, go to 127 instead.

59

After they had paid him the five-coin fine, the Goth offered to give them a lift to the next exit of the chariotway. 'I just don't understand these Goths,' Asterix remarked when they were walking along a much quieter road again. 'First, they nearly run us down, next they charge us a heavy fine and then they give us a lift!' *Go to 157.*

60

The mountain road for Bergomum had only gone a couple of miles or so, however, when it became blocked by a huge avalanche. So the Gauls returned to Octodurus, deciding to try the road for Dertona instead. After a quick snack at a mountain inn (a bowl of muesli for Asterix and Dogmatix, and an entire herd of roast mountain goat for Obelix), the Gauls soon reached the Italian frontier. The frontier post was heavily guarded by Romans, though, and so Asterix decided he had better take one of his magic potions. A brief fight later and the Gauls were quietly crossing into Italia. 'These frontier formalities are such a nuisance!' Asterix remarked as he straightened his helmet.

Remove a MAGIC POTION CARD from ASTERIX'S WAIST-SLIT. Now go to 220. (Remember: when there are no magic potion cards left in Asterix's waist-slit their mission has to stop, and you must start the game again.)

61

It was Dogmatix who went through the turnstile first, able to slip underneath while the other two struggled with the silly bars. 'It's all your fault,' Asterix told his friend crossly. 'If you weren't so fat, we wouldn't have got stuck!' Anyway, they were finally all on the other side and, after climbing a great number of stone steps, they realised what the place was. 'Why, it's a circus,' Asterix exclaimed as they looked down on the arena far below, '– for gladiator fights and throwing people to the lions!' They had just taken their seats to watch the first event, however, when a Roman officer shouted something at them from his box behind. 'You don't have a translator with you, do you?' Asterix whispered to his friend. 'He sounds as if he might cause trouble!'

If OBELIX does have a TRANSLATOR, use it to find out what the Roman was shouting by translating the content of his speech-balloon below. If not, go to 229 instead.

Handing the cobbler the thirteen coins, Asterix said it was worth every one of them – you had to pay for fine craftsmanship in these days of shoddy goods! He then asked the cobbler how it was that he could understand their language. 'Well, to tell you the truth, I'm a Gaul myself really,' the cobbler confessed. 'It's just better for business if I pretend I'm Roman!' He went on to explain how he had moved to Italia many years ago, learning the language with the help of a translator. 'But I'm pretty fluent now,' he added, 'so perhaps you would like the translator yourselves?'

If OBELIX doesn't already carry it, put the TRANSLATOR into his WAIST-SLIT. Now go to 79.

63

'No, I don't think *JUPITER* is right,' said the guard, scratching his head while he had a think about it. 'Just wait there a minute while I go and ask someone!' Of course, the Gauls didn't wait, cheekily strolling through the unguarded gates as soon as the guard had gone. 'I sometimes wonder why we bother trying to be cunning with the Romans,' Asterix chuckled. 'A lot of them don't seem to have a brain in their heads!' *Go to 14.*

64

The steps went deeper and deeper into the ground as Dogmatix led his two friends down. Suddenly, though, he started to make a concerned yapping noise. His path had been blocked by a dozen or so large Roman guards! When they asked the Gauls what they were doing, Asterix replied that they were doctors, going to give Getafix a check-up before he was taken out to the lions. 'We must make sure his heart's strong enough to stand the ordeal,' he said, thinking quickly. 'The spectators get very disappointed when the victim just collapses right at the beginning!' The Romans weren't altogether convinced by this explanation, however, asking them what the official password was.

Does OBELIX have a PASSWORD SCROLL with him? If so,

use it to find out the correct password by placing it exactly over the scroll shape below – then follow the appropriate instruction. If he doesn't have one, you'll have to guess which instruction to follow.

If you think it's SHIELD   go to 123
If you think it's HELMET   go to 191
If you think it's ARMOUR   go to 24

Following the fisherman's direction, our Gaulish friends arrived at a raft crossing-point about half a mile further along the river. 'If you intend travelling right across Europe,' the raft-operator told them as he ferried them across, 'you're going to need a translator to work out what people of other nationalities are saying. Since you're Gauls like myself, I'm happy to give you one free of charge.'

If OBELIX doesn't already carry it, put the TRANSLATOR into his WAIST-SLIT. Now go to 55.

66

The three travellers now left Noviodunum, taking the road towards the town of Araines. 'I wish the Romans wouldn't build their roads so straight,' Asterix complained as they were walking along. 'It makes them so boring!' At that, Obelix's face suddenly started to brighten up. 'Talking of boring . . .' he began but Asterix quickly shut him up, knowing that he was about to get on to his favourite subject. 'No, we don't have time to go for a little boar-hunting!' he told him sternly. They had only walked a few miles further when they noticed several armed men creeping stealthily along in the shadow of a wall in front of them. Realising that they had been seen, the men gave what sounded like an order, but as they were speaking in another tongue it would need a translator to work out what the order was.

If OBELIX carries a TRANSLATOR, use it to find out what the

men were saying by translating the instruction in the speech-balloon below. If he doesn't, go to 100 instead.

67

Now leaving Alesia, the Gauls started on their journey again. Many miles later, their road reached a bridge, but they couldn't cross because it was occupied by a mass of striking slaves. 'We're sitting here until the Romans restore our overtime,' their leader, Flyingpicix, told them. 'We demand our rights,' he continued. Asterix tried to point out that there wasn't any advantage in overtime when they weren't paid for the work, but Flyingpicix insisted that it was the principle of the thing. So it looked as if the Gauls were just going to have to *swim* across the river, Asterix leading the way down to the water's edge.

Throw the special DICE to decide who is to reach the other side of the river first.

If you throw ASTERIX   go to 280
If you throw OBELIX   go to 186
If you throw DOGMATIX   go to 5

When he had paid the chalet-owner the seventeen coins, Obelix asked him for fifty rashers of Danish boar and a small slice of fried bread. But the chalet-owner told them that boar was hard to get hold of in the mountains and he would bring them some Helvetian cheese instead. Asterix and Dogmatix found the cheese very tasty but Obelix kept complaining that it was full of holes. 'Well, at least you've now got several holes in your stomach instead of just the one you had before!' Asterix chuckled. They were now about to leave the chalet to continue on their journey but, before they went, the owner offered them a password scroll. 'You'll soon be crossing the frontier into Italia,' he told them, 'and you might well need it!'

If OBELIX doesn't already have it, put the PASSWORD SCROLL into his WAIST-SLIT. Now go to 84.

'Er . . . it's something not very friendly!' Asterix tried, being forced to guess what the Roman was saying. Switching back to Gaulish again, though, the Roman told him that he was wrong – it *had* been friendly. 'Oh, in that case you won't want to fight us!' Asterix replied cheekily but the Roman and his friends suddenly circled them. The little Gaul just had time to drink one of his magic potions before the punch-up began. 'I wonder whether those groans of theirs are in Latin or Gaulish?' Asterix asked his friend with a chuckle, a few clonks and blams later!

Remove a MAGIC POTION CARD from ASTERIX'S WAIST-SLIT. Now go to 77.

'That look's like them!' Asterix suddenly exclaimed, pointing to a building with steam coming out of the top, and he hurriedly led the way up the broad steps. Sure enough, it *was* the baths and, after a good freshen-up, they were ready to continue their journey again. Instead of walking, though, Asterix had the clever idea of hiding in the back of one of three carts about to set off from a toga factory. The trouble was – which should they choose? The togas in the first cart were labelled for Luca, in the second for Patavium, and the third for Eporedia. 'Unless you've got a map with you,' Asterix told his friend, 'we'll just have to make a guess!'

If OBELIX does have a MAP, use it to find out which of the three towns below is in the right direction for Rome from Dertona – then follow the appropriate instruction. If he doesn't, you'll have to guess which instruction to follow.

If you think it's LUCA go to 239
If you think it's PATAVIUM go to 214
If you think it's EPOREDIA go to 147

71

As soon as they had paid the three coins, the guards waved the Gauls past. 'Honestly, these Romans are getting very corrupt,' Asterix commented as they approached the palace doors. 'I wouldn't be surprised if one day it leads to their Empire's downfall!' Obelix asked whether they should inform Caesar of the guards' corruption but Asterix replied that he didn't think it was a very good idea. 'Those guards might be stupid enough to think that we're decorators,' he said, 'but I doubt that Caesar will be!' *Go to 34.*

72

The two Gauls wandered through the muddy streets of Noviodunum, looking for somewhere to rest and to enquire about Getafix. Every time they asked a passer-by where the nearest inn was, however, they were met by a sudden stream of abuse. 'They don't seem to like strangers very much!' Asterix exclaimed, becoming scared to open his mouth. So they decided they would just have to find an inn without a passer-by's help, wondering who would spot it first.

Throw the special DICE to find out.

If you throw ASTERIX	go to 56
If you throw OBELIX	go to 2
If you throw DOGMATIX	go to 201

'Well, what's this information you have?' Asterix asked the peasant as soon as he had handed him the eleven coins. The peasant told him that the Druid had been brought past his hut four days ago and he had overheard his captives say that when they got him to Rome they were going to make him reveal the secret of the magic potion. 'Mmm, so the rumours are correct,' Asterix considered anxiously when the peasant had finished. 'Let's just hope we reach Rome in time!' *Go to 66.*

'Look, there they are!' Asterix suddenly exclaimed, pointing to some hazy mountain tops in the far distance. They had only walked a few miles closer to the Alps when they noticed there was a Roman checkpoint ahead. As they joined the end of the queue waiting to pass through, Asterix told his friend that they must be leaving Gaul and crossing the frontier into Helvetia (the Roman name for Switzerland). It was at last their turn to move up to the checkpoint but the Romans said that they could only walk through if they knew the password (passports hadn't been invented yet!).

Does OBELIX carry a PASSWORD SCROLL with him? If so, use it to find out the correct password by placing exactly over the

scroll shape below – then follow the appropriate instruction. If he doesn't have one, you'll have to guess which instruction to follow.

If you think it's JUPITER	go to 251
If you think it's MERCURY	go to 274
If you think it's NEPTUNE	go to 18

'Ah, we tricked you,' the Romans mocked as they told them they had got the password wrong. 'I bet you thought it was *NEPTUNE* because he's the god of the sea!' They then ordered the Gauls to come with them to work the oars at the bottom of their galley, along with the rest of the slaves. 'We're sentencing you to thirty years down there,' they told them. 'It's damp, hot, infested with rats and the job's a real bore!' At the mention of boar, Obelix was ready to go along but Asterix started to drink one of his magic potions. 'You can row your own galley!' Asterix was soon shouting at the Romans over the side as they were floundering only half-conscious in the water.

*Remove a **MAGIC POTION CARD** from **ASTERIX'S WAIST-SLIT**. Now go to 167.*

76

Fortunately, Obelix *did* have a coinbag and they paid the ticket-man the eight coins. Before he went on to the next passenger, Asterix asked the man why some Helvetians spoke Gaulish and some didn't. 'That's because we speak several languages in Helvetia,' the man told him. 'Some speak Helvetian-Gaulish, some speak Helvetian-Latin and some speak Helvetian-Goth!' He then offered them a translator to make travelling through Helvetia a little easier.

*If **OBELIX** doesn't already carry it, put the **TRANSLATOR** into his **WAIST-SLIT**. Now go to 20.*

77

After a good night's sleep at the inn, the Gauls continued on their journey, eventually reaching the city of Dertona. Wandering through the crowded streets, they noticed lots of people heading for a huge oval-shaped building in the centre. 'Perhaps there's a big feast going on inside?' Obelix suggested hopefully, and so they decided to make for the building themselves. There were long queues leading back from the building, however, and it was a good half-hour before they finally reached one of the entrances. 'Only one at a time,' the official told them at the wooden turnstile. 'Now which of you is going to pass through first?'

Throw the special DICE to decide.

If you throw ASTERIX	go to 43
If you throw OBELIX	go to 121
If you throw DOGMATIX	go to 61

78

'It's a good job you had a coinbag with you,' Asterix told his friend as they paid the slave the six coins, 'otherwise they might have insisted on making us dirty again!' As they left the baths, Asterix added that it could have been even worse – the owners might have had them thrown to the lions. 'Or even worse still,' Obelix said with a shiver, 'they might have dropped us in that really cold pool!' **Go to 52.**

Ready to leave Narnia, the Gauls noticed that there were three roads they could take. One went to Populonia, one to Falerii and one to Cosa. 'Why is it always three roads we have to choose from, instead of just one?' Obelix complained. But Asterix said the game wouldn't be as much fun otherwise!

Does OBELIX have a MAP with him? If so, use it to find out which of the three towns below is in the right direction for Rome from Narnia – then follow the appropriate instruction. If he doesn't have one, you'll have to guess which instruction to follow.

If you think it's POPULONIA	go to 23
If you think it's FALERII	go to 160
If you think it's COSA	go to 106

80

Since they didn't have any money with them, the Gauls decided they would just have to bash the cell door open. So Obelix took a long run at it, ramming it with his shoulder. The door was so thick and heavily bolted, however, that it still remained in place. Obelix was just about to take another run at it when the guards inside started shouting for help. Within seconds, the Gauls could hear what sounded like thousands of feet coming towards them from above. 'I think we might have a bit of trouble on our hands!' Asterix remarked with concern . . . *Go to 221.*

81

After buying provisions at the town, the Gauls spent the next three days on the road so they would get as many miles behind them as possible. Fortunately, the nights were very warm and so sleeping out was no hardship. On the evening of the third day, however, a thunderstorm broke out and they looked for a roadside inn for shelter. 'There's one!' Asterix suddenly exclaimed, pointing to a large stone hut a few hundred metres ahead. The storm was making them so wet that they all ran the short distance.

Throw the special DICE to decide who is to reach the inn first.

If you throw ASTERIX	go to 99
If you throw OBELIX	go to 175
If you throw DOGMATIX	go to 232

Handing the soothsayer the nine coins, Obelix eagerly waited for him to analyse his huge plate of boar bones. 'Well, will our mission be successful or not?' he asked impatiently as the strange-looking man began to scratch his head. The soothsayer confessed that the bones weren't all that clear on the matter but they did reveal that Obelix was a man of great appetite. 'That's incredible!' Obelix exclaimed with delight all over his face. 'For a moment, I thought you might just be a fraud!' *Go to 39.*

The Gauls had been walking along the Tolosa road for a quite a way when they caught up with a large herd of cattle. 'I'm taking them down to Hispania, to the arena,' the owner told them, brandishing a stick every once in a while. 'They have this silly game down there where they wave red rags at them!' He was just about to explain the rules of the game, and how a blue or yellow rag wasn't quite as good, when the Gauls suddenly turned back the way they had come. If this was the road for Hispania, then they were obviously going in the wrong direction! *Go to 111.*

Their journey through Helvetia continued, the Gauls eventually reaching the mountain town of Octodurus. They were going to look for somewhere to eat there but all the inns were packed with people for the annual yodelling contest. 'Oh, what a racket!' Asterix exclaimed with his hands over his ears as the competitors' voices echoed round the valley. 'It's not much better than Cacofonix's singing!' They decided to press on for the next village, therefore, and found that three mountain roads left from Octodurus. One went towards Bergomum, one towards Vindonissa and the third towards Dertona. 'I wonder which we take?' Asterix asked.

Does OBELIX have a MAP with him? If so, use it to find out which of the three towns below is in the right direction for Rome from Octodurus – then follow the appropriate instruction. If he doesn't have one, you'll have to guess which instruction to follow.

If you think it's BERGOMUM   go to 60
If you think it's VINDONISSA   go to 137
If you think it's DERTONA   go to 30

85

Having paid the innkeeper the money, the Gauls quickly slipped into the Roman uniforms. Fortunately, the uniforms were both about their size – one big and one small – and so the Gauls looked fairly convincing when the Romans entered the inn. Obelix had great difficulty trying not to giggle, however, and Asterix had to keep kicking him under the table. For one tense moment, it looked as if the leader of the Romans had heard him . . . because he came over to their table. But it was only to hand them out a map for their next invasion. 'And hold your stomach in, man!' he added to Obelix. 'You're bursting out of your uniform!'

If OBELIX doesn't already carry it, put the MAP into his WAIST-SLIT. Now go to 77.

86

When the galley-owner found out that the Gauls didn't have any money for their fare, he immediately started shouting for a Roman patrol. The patrol soon arrived – about twenty soldiers in all – and they prepared to board the galley to arrest the Gauls. While Asterix was hurriedly drinking one of his magic potions, Obelix noticed that the front of the galley was loaded up with hundreds and hundreds of water-melons. Asterix suddenly saw them too and, shortly after, they were both pelting them at the Romans! 'One point if you knock them over and two points if you knock them out!' the little Gaul suggested spiritedly as the melons splattered on the Romans' helmets. At exactly fifteen points each, there was only one soldier standing . . . but he suddenly slipped on all the mess and knocked himself out. So the game had to remain a draw!

Remove a *MAGIC POTION CARD* from *ASTERIX'S WAIST SLIT*. Now go to 149.

87

When the Gauls found the dungeons, they immediately started looking for cell number seven. '. . . Four . . . five . . . six . . .,' they read out as they passed the doors – and finally they reached it! Peering through the little barred window, however, they saw that there was a guard on the other side. 'We've come to take Getafix up to the arena,' Asterix called out, trying to disguise his voice. The guard became suspicious, however, saying that he would only open the cell door when they gave the correct password.

Does *OBELIX* have a *PASSWORD SCROLL* with him? If so, use it to find out the correct password by placing exactly over the

scroll shape below – then follow the appropriate instruction. If he
doesn't, you'll have to guess which instruction to follow.

If you think it's JUPITER   go to 140
If you think it's MERCURY   go to 116
If you think it's NEPTUNE   go to 181

88

The two Gauls had obviously made a bad guess with *DAGGER*,
however, because the man's face grew even more hostile than it was
before. But then he suddenly seemed to recognise Asterix's face.
'By Jupiter, you're the famous Asterix, aren't you?' he asked. 'I've
seen carvings of you on Roman "wanted" slabs!' This very much

changed his attitude towards them and he was soon warmly showing them the best sleeping-quarters he had. Obelix didn't look quite as happy as the other two, though. He thought *his* face should be on Roman 'wanted' slabs as well! ***Go to 203.***

89

'Rubbish!' exclaimed the sentry when they had guessed at *DAGGER* as the password. Asterix pretended to misunderstand, though, indignantly protesting that he hadn't dropped any rubbish! 'No, I mean your password is rubbish,' the sentry said, trying to make himself clear. So Asterix now changed his password from *DAGGER* to *RUBBISH*, asking to be let past. 'No, I didn't mean that *RUBBISH* was the password,' explained the sentry, 'I meant that *DAGGER* was rubbish. But *RUBBISH* is rubbish as well!' He had made himself so confused at this point, however, that he decided just to wave the Gauls through! ***Go to 154.***

90

Impatiently reading through his translator, Obelix found out that Dogmatix had been arrested for not carrying a dog licence! 'The Roman says that it is against the town law,' Obelix told his friend with indignation, 'and any dog without a licence has to be locked up!' The overgrown Gaul disliked the Romans enough at the best of times but something like this made him grow purple with hostility. Little wonder that the soldiers coyly gave him back his dog and then suddenly ran off in all directions! ***Go to 67.***

Their journey into Helvetia continued, and the Gauls eventually arrived at the shores of a large lake surrounded by mountains. 'We're going to have to try and find a way to get to the other side,' said Asterix. 'Let's see if there's a ferry anywhere.' So they started walking along the shore, Obelix suddenly spotting a large raft a little further round. Since it looked as if it was about to cast off, they all hurried up to the gangplank.

Throw the special DICE to decide who is to reach the gangplank first.

If you throw ASTERIX	go to 212
If you throw OBELIX	go to 145
If you throw DOGMATIX	go to 114

'They want to take possession of our galley,' Obelix translated for everyone as the pirates began to get impatient, '. . . and they would like us to walk the plank!' There was then a hurried search for a plank on the galley but there wasn't a single one to be found. As the pirates grew more and more angry, Asterix pointed to a plank on their own ship, suggesting they use that. They seemed to think it was a good idea, crossing back and immediately starting to prise the plank out. Asterix had deliberately selected one along the ship's side, however – just on the water-line – and both it and the pirates rapidly began to sink! *Go to 167.*

It was no surprise to the other two that it was Obelix who sampled the pizzas first! Watching him eat, one of a group of Romans at the next table politely asked what he thought of it. 'Well, a slice or two of boar might improve it a bit . . .' Obelix began but then the Roman suddenly drew out his sword. He said that he had been speaking in Gaulish and that it was a trick he used to find out if suspects were spies or not. Asterix quickly explained that they were scholars, saying that Gaulish was just one of the many foreign languages they studied. The Roman was not fully convinced, though, and followed them outside. Asking them what he was saying next, he suddenly started gabbling away in Latin!

Does OBELIX have a TRANSLATOR with him? If so, use it to find out what the Roman was saying by translating the content of his speech-balloon below. If he doesn't, go to 69 instead.

Shyly covering himself up as he scanned through his translator at the edge of the baths, Obelix gradually went blue with anger. The attendant was telling them that there were no dogs allowed in the water! He quickly helped Asterix and Dogmatix out and then took a long run at the bath, leaping into the air. The pool was completely emptied . . . astonished bathers suddenly finding themselves standing on the dry bottom! 'If Dogmatix can't go in the water, then no one can!' Obelix remarked huffily as the Gauls went through the exit. *Go to 52.*

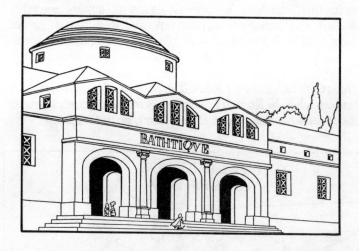

95

They had only followed the Arretium road for a mile when it suddenly ended. 'Typical,' Asterix exclaimed with his hands on his hips, '– they haven't finished it yet! They're so busy conquering neighbouring countries that they can't even get their own roads completed!' So they just had to turn back for Cosa, deciding on the Falerii road this time. As they were walking along, Asterix suddenly tripped over Obelix's big feet. 'Oh no, you've made me burst one of my gourds of magic potion!' he cried as the precious liquid seeped into the ground.

Remove a MAGIC POTION CARD from ASTERIX'S WAIST-SLIT. Now go to 149.

'They're saying that they've never known such an awkward old man,' Obelix whispered, scanning up and down the translator as the Romans chatted away, '. . . and now they're complaining about his long beard. They kept tripping up on it!' Finding it difficult to stifle their laughter, the Gauls decided they had better leave, soon being on their way again. 'Well, at least we now know that Getafix was in good spirits!' Asterix chuckled as they followed the road south. *Go to 117.*

Asterix hadn't led them far down the steps when a number of Roman guards appeared, demanding to know where they were going. 'We just wanted to say goodbye to one of our friends before he's thrown to the lions,' Asterix explained innocently. The guards said that visitors were forbidden, though, and that they would just have to shout goodbye to him from the stadium. 'But he won't be able to hear us above all the cheering,' Asterix objected, and so the guards had a secret discussion with each other. They eventually agreed to let them visit their friend for a bribe of fifteen coins!

Does OBELIX have a COINBAG with him? If so, 'count out' the fifteen coins by rotating the disc – then go to the number that appears on the other side. If he doesn't have one, go to 12 instead.

'That isn't the right password,' the centurion exclaimed, immediately beginning to raise the alarm, 'you're obviously spies!' Within seconds the Gauls were surrounded by a handful of muscular Romans but the soldiers couldn't understand why the big fat one was rubbing his hands with glee. 'I just feel like a bit of gentle exercise,' Obelix beamed, and he and his little friend were suddenly right in the middle of the soldiers, fists flying! The Romans were soon sent reeling to the ground but one or two of them had been tougher than Asterix thought and it had sapped his strength a little. 'I'd better take a gourd of magic potion just to be on the safe side,' he said.

Remove a _MAGIC POTION CARD_ from _ASTERIX'S WAIST-SLIT_. Now go to 72.

Asterix reached the inn first, knocking on the door while he waited for the others to arrive. When the door was opened, however, he saw that the place was run by Romans. 'Only friends of Rome may stay here, barbarian,' the pompous owner told him. 'Now get back into the storm where you belong!' Although Asterix didn't really fancy the idea of spending the night with Romans, he didn't fancy catching a cold either and so he said he _was_ a friend of Rome. 'If that be the case,' said the innkeeper, looking down his Roman nose at him, 'then you should know the password. Tell me what it is!'

Does _OBELIX_ carry a _PASSWORD SCROLL_ with him? If so,

use it to find out the correct password by placing exactly over the scroll shape below – then follow the appropriate instruction. If he doesn't have one, you'll have to guess which instruction to follow.

```
    E H L     F F E  B
  B D A  J M T   9 N L
    I   E U S F   O 2
   O G P N L   B L H
  D E I E   I A   B R
   P N R Q U 4 R   9
     H  S O I C E
   B      F 3 T A 9 M
  S O A U B !    E
    B A U     C S N
  D 8 O H B A 2 Z
```

If you think it's AUGUSTUS   go to 244
If you think it's JULIUS   go to 273
If you think it's TIBERIUS   go to 163

100

Since Obelix didn't have a translator, the Gauls just had to ignore the men's order and politely waved them aside so they could get past. The men (who were really ruthless bandits) were so taken aback by their calmness that they meekly obliged, their clubs dropping to the ground. 'I do hope they didn't think us too rude!' Obelix remarked innocently as they continued on their way. *Go to 154.*

101

'In that case you must turn back!' the Roman told them when Obelix said that they didn't have any coins. Seeing that the Gauls intended to take no notice of his order, he then sent out a carrier-pigeon for reinforcements. 'Hurry up, pigeon,' Obelix muttered anxiously into the sky as they waited for the message to be received, 'I just feel like a nice fight!' At last the message got through, and Asterix drank one of his magic potions as he spotted the dozen or so reinforcements hurrying towards them out of the distance. It wasn't long, of course, before they were sent flying back into the distance . . . and the Gauls quietly resumed their journey!

Remove a MAGIC POTION CARD from ASTERIX'S WAIST-SLIT. Now go to 128.

'Come on – wake up, wake up,' Obelix bellowed to his two friends as the morning sun came pouring through the chalet window. 'We don't want to miss breakfast!' They all finally walked into the breakfast room, Obelix saying he was so hungry that he felt as if he had a great big hole in his stomach. 'A few rashers of crispy Danish boar would soon put it right, though,' he smiled as they sat down at a wooden table. When the chalet-owner came to take their order, however, he politely reminded them that they hadn't paid yet and that the cost of the bed and breakfast for all three of them would be seventeen coins!

Does OBELIX have a COINBAG with him? If so, use it to 'count out' the seventeen coins by rotating the disc – then go to the number that appears on the other side. If he doesn't, go to 148 instead.

Boarding the galley for Massilia, the Gauls asked the captain if it would be sailing towards Italia. He told them that Massilia was the other direction, though, and they should have taken the Albingaunum galley. So the three friends ran after the Albingaunum galley but, by the time they had reached its mooring place, it had set sail! 'Let's try and swim for it!' Asterix suggested and they all plunged into the sea, Dogmatix sitting on Obelix's tummy as the two Gauls did a furious backstroke. They at last reached the galley, scrambling up the side. The swim had made Asterix so exhausted, however, that he had to take one of his magic potions to restore his strength – especially since Italia, the land of the Romans, was soon in view!

Remove a _MAGIC POTION CARD_ from _ASTERIX'S WAIST-SLIT. Now go to 220._ (Remember: when there are no magic potion cards left in Asterix's waist-slit their mission has to stop, and you must start the game again.)

104

The Gauls' journey through Italia continued and, at the end of their third day in the country, they reached the seaside town of Populonia. Since time was running desperately short, Asterix suggested they take an overnight galley so they could be travelling while they slept. None of the galleys went all the way to Rome but they did find one that went to Cosa, which was in the right direction for the imperial city. The merchant who owned the galley welcomed them aboard and then led them below to their hammocks.

Throw the special _DICE_ to decide who is to jump into their hammock first.

If you throw ASTERIX   go to 222
If you throw OBELIX   go to 189
If you throw DOGMATIX   go to 268

The Gauls could immediately tell that *SWORD* was wrong and so they all ran for the door before the Goths advanced any further. Asterix's reason for fleeing was that he didn't want to waste one of his magic potions but he couldn't understand why Obelix hadn't wished to fight either. 'I didn't want to spoil that lovely cream cake!' his friend informed him with his stupid grin. As it turned out, though, Asterix might just as well have used one of his magic potions after all because a gourd suddenly slipped from his belt, spilling all its contents on the ground!

*Remove a **MAGIC POTION CARD** from **ASTERIX'S WAIST-SLIT**. Now go to 157.*

Our three frinds had only gone a very short way along the Cosa road when they spotted what looked like the whole of the Roman army coming from the other direction! 'By Jupiter, there are millions of them,' Asterix exclaimed. 'There must be at least twenty or thirty legions there!' Obelix was quite happy to try and take them on but Asterix said that there were far too many even for him. So they decided to turn back for Narnia and take the Falerii road instead. *Go to 45.*

Walking through a maze of underground tunnels, the Gauls at last reached the dungeons. They immediately began looking for cell seven, reading the numbers on the doors. 'Here it is!' Asterix exclaimed, but, when he peered in through the little barred window, he saw that there was a guard on the other side. 'We'll have to try and trick him into opening the door,' Asterix whispered to his friend, starting to think of a plan. He decided to pretend that they had lost their way to the stadium, asking the guard if he could show them where to go. The guard replied that it would mean leaving his post, though, and he would only take that risk for twelve coins!

Does OBELIX have a COINBAG with him? If so, 'count out' the twelve coins by rotating the disc – then go to the number that appears in the window on the other side. If he doesn't, go to 80 instead.

'What can I get you?' the innkeeper asked when the travellers had sat down on a stone bench. 'Today's my birthday and so all drinks are on the house.' Obelix thanked him for his generosity but said he was much too tired to climb on to the roof for his drink. 'No, *on the house* means that they are free,' Asterix explained to his confused friend, with a bit of a sigh. The three of them had a think for a moment, considering what they would like.

Throw the special DICE to decide who is to order first.

If you throw ASTERIX	go to 272
If you throw OBELIX	go to 217
If you throw DOGMATIX	go to 262

109

After they had passed their ninth milestone on the way to Caesaromagus, they decided to stop at a roadside inn for a bit of refreshment. As soon as Obelix had sunk his teeth into his roast boar, however, he realised they had come the wrong way. 'It must have been one of those other roads that went south,' he told his friend expertly. 'You only get boar tasting as delicious as this in the very north of Gaul!' So they made the long journey back, taking one of the other roads this time. *Go to 16.*

110

As they were walking along the road to Gennes, the Gauls caught up with a large cart full of people in bright straw hats. When Asterix asked them where they were going, they said that they were on their holidays and they were taking the cart to the seaside. 'If this road leads to the seaside,' Asterix remarked with dismay, turning back to Obelix, 'that means we must be going the wrong way. The road for Rome would point inland!' They therefore set off across the fields hoping to meet the road they should have taken in the first place. *Go to 154.*

111

The travellers at last reached the very south of Gaul, spotting the blue Mediterranean. Everywhere they looked, there were warriors lying on the sand – many of them without helmets. 'I'm not sure I approve of this topless bathing!' Asterix said prudishly as they walked along. They were having a short rest under some palm trees when Asterix noticed a galley about to set sail along the coast. 'It looks as if it's going to Italia,' Asterix told his two friends hurriedly. 'Come on, it will be much easier than walking!' So the Gauls yelled at the galley to wait, running towards the gangplank.

Throw the special DICE to decide who is to reach the galley first.

If you throw ASTERIX go to 219
If you throw OBELIX go to 238
If you throw DOGMATIX go to 40

112

When the Gauls told him that they didn't have any coins with them, the Goths ordered them all to climb into his chariot so he could transport them to gaol. Obelix was about to punch him on the nose but Asterix whispered to him to wait, saying they might as well have a free lift first. They at last reached the gaol and Asterix secretly drank one of his magic potions as half a dozen Goth soldiers came to escort them to their cells. Moments later, four of them were out cold on the ground and the other two were fleeing for the cells themselves, bolting the doors from the inside! 'I thought it was *us* they wanted to lock up!' Obelix remarked with a confused scratch of his head.

Remove a MAGIC POTION CARD from ASTERIX'S WAIST-SLIT. Now go to 157.

113

Always very fond of water, it was Dogmatix who spotted the baths first, suddenly giving little yaps. Entering the large, colonnaded building, the Gauls immediately made for the warmest of the various pools. 'I don't know how those Romans can stand that icy-cold one,' Asterix remarked as they floated in the heated water. 'I always said they were crazy!' When they felt thoroughly washed, they then went into the massage room to have their muscles soothed by a huge slave called Therapeutix. 'Now let me see,' the slave said when he had finished. 'That's a heated bath, a back massage and a neck massage . . . that will be six coins in all!' The Gauls had completely forgotten that it would cost money!

Does OBELIX have a COINBAG with him? If so 'count out' the six coins by rotating the disc – then turn to the number that appears on the other side. If he doesn't, go to 283 instead.

114

Dogmatix reached the gangplank first, stubbornly sitting on it so the raft couldn't cast off until his two friends had arrived. When they had reached the opposite shore of the lake, they saw that there was a choice of three roads they could follow. The first went to a town called Brigantium, the second to a town called Bergomum and the third to a town called Vindonissa. 'We want the one that is the most southerly of the three,' said Asterix, scratching his head, and he asked Obelix if he had a map to help them decide.

If OBELIX does have a MAP, use it to find out which of the three towns below is the farthest south – then go to the appropriate number. If he doesn't, you'll have to guess which number to go to.

If you think it's BRIGANTIUM	go to 282
If you think it's BERGOMUM	go to 156
If you think it's VINDONISSA	go to 50

115

'Wrong, wrong, wrong!' the guards replied to their guess at *AUGUSTUS*, all dancing about delightedly. Still dancing about, they drew out their swords ready to arrest the Gauls. 'I suppose it's pretty rare for anything exciting to happen in their job,' Asterix tried to explain their reaction as he drank one of his magic potions.

Moments later, though, and life was even more exciting for the guards . . . the Gauls having thumped them into the air! 'Yes, you have to be sympathetic,' Asterix added as they now casually approached the palace doors. 'Life must be very boring just standing about doing nothing all day!'

Remove a *MAGIC POTION CARD* from *ASTERIX'S WAIST-SLIT*. Now go to 34.

116

'Are you positive it's *MERCURY*?' the guard called back from behind the cell door. Asterix wasn't sure whether to change to something else or not but he eventually decided the guard was just trying to trick him and so stuck with *MERCURY* as the password. 'Well, it's wrong!' the guard replied triumphantly. 'You're obviously Gauls come to help the Druid escape!' And, with that, he suddenly raised the alarm, his voice echoing through the entire length of the dungeons. Within seconds, the Gauls could hear hundreds of feet running towards them from above. 'It sounds as if the whole of the Roman army is coming!' Asterix remarked with concern . . . ***Go to 221.***

The two Gauls and their dog at last reached the town of Araines, looking for somewhere to sleep for the night. 'Perhaps there will be a B and B place somewhere,' said Asterix, checking all the huts for a sign on the door. Obelix had a big smile on his face, thinking B and B must stand for Boar and Bed. Dogmatix also had a smile, thinking it stood for Bone and Bed! Guessing their thoughts, Asterix was about to correct them both but then he realised they might not look so hard and therefore decided to keep quiet.

Throw the special DICE to see who is to spot the B and B sign first.

If you throw ASTERIX	go to 208
If you throw OBELIX	go to 183
If you throw DOGMATIX	go to 236

When the sentry had told them that *JAVELIN* was the right password and let them through the gates, Obelix looked a little disappointed. 'I quite wanted to go to the circus,' he grumbled when Asterix asked him what was the matter. But Asterix said that the circus the Roman was talking about was not one that you watched but where you were thrown to the lions. 'I know,' said Obelix with his head still down. 'I've always wanted to stroke a lion!' ***Go to 154.***

119

'Look, there's an Alp!' Obelix exclaimed, suddenly noticing a hazy mountain top in the distance. 'And there's another one . . . and another one!' It wasn't long before their road crossed the frontier into Helvetia (the Roman name for Switzerland) and, after having to knock out the odd sentry or two at the barrier, they entered this beautiful country. They finally reached the town of Aventicum where the road divided three ways. The first branch went to Octodurus, the second to Vesontio and the third to Augustodunum. Asterix asked his friend if he had a map with him so they would know which to take.

If OBELIX does have a map, use it to find out which of the three towns below is in the right direction for Rome from Aventicum – then follow the appropriate instruction. If he doesn't, you'll have to guess which instruction to follow.

If you think it's OCTODURUS	go to 258
If you think it's VESONTIO	go to 281
If you think it's AUGUSTODUNUM	go to 237

120

It didn't take long before the galley arrived at its destination of Albingaunum and the Gauls could see from all the Roman officials ashore that they had at last reached Italia! 'Anything to declare – wine, sundials, precious menhirs?' one of the Romans asked. 'Or some distilled myrtleberry juice, perhaps?' Obelix replied that they only had gourds of magic potion with them, however, and honestly went on to describe how they enabled his friend to take on dozens of Romans at a time. 'Well, I can't see magic potion on the customs list,' the Roman told them officiously, 'so I suppose it's okay!' *Go to 220.*

121

Obelix was so full of excitement that the others thought they had better let *him* go through the turnstile first. He led the way up a series of steps to the top of a vast stadium. 'Oh, now I know what this is,' said Asterix. 'It's a circus, where they have gladiator fights!' The Gauls found watching the fights rather boring, though – thinking it wasn't nearly as much fun as doing the fighting yourself! – and so left well before the end. As they left the town they weren't sure which of the three roads just outside they should take; the Eporedia road, the Patavium road or the Luca road. 'I hope you've got a map with you,' Asterix said to his friend, 'or we'll just have to make a guess!'

If OBELIX does have a MAP with him, use it to find out which of the three towns below is in the right direction for Rome from Dertona – then follow the appropriate instruction. If he doesn't have one, you'll have to guess which instruction to follow.

If you think it's EPOREDIA	go to 132
If you think it's PATAVIUM	go to 284
If you think it's LUCA	go to 247

'He's telling the other person that he thinks we're Gaulish spies,' Obelix whispered, reading his translator by the light of the candle. '. . . And now he's saying that, when we come down for breakfast in the morning, he's going to have the house full of Roman soldiers so they can arrest us.' At this, Obelix rubbed his hands together, telling Asterix that he always enjoyed a good fight just before breakfast – to work up his appetite! But Asterix said it might be better to avoid any trouble and so, very early next morning, the Gauls crept out before anyone was awake. As they were continuing on their journey, Asterix suddenly noticed that Dogmatix had something in his mouth. 'Look, it's a password scroll,' he exclaimed. 'Dogmatix must have found it in our room!'

*If **OBELIX** doesn't already have it, put the **PASSWORD SCROLL** into his **WAIST-SLIT**. Now go to 45.*

123

'No, the password isn't *SHIELD*!' the Romans screamed at them, and immediately drew their swords. Obelix scratched his head for a moment before bending down towards his friend. 'Does that mean they don't believe we're doctors!' he asked in confusion. But Asterix was too busy drinking one of his magic potions – and then knocking all the Romans down the steps! 'You might have left me one!' Obelix complained sulkily as he suddenly realised that the fight was already over.

Remove a _MAGIC POTION CARD_ from _ASTERIX'S WAIST-SLIT_. _Now go to 107_. (Remember: when there are no magic potion cards left in Asterix's waist-slit their mission has to stop, and you must start the game again.)

124

Obelix's choice of road soon ran alongside a large wood. Thinking there might be some wild boar (his favourite food!) in there, Obelix suggested that they go for a little detour but it wasn't long before they were well and truly lost. 'Now, how do we find our way out again?' Asterix asked his friend crossly. Suddenly, though, Dogmatix's ears started to prick up and, seconds later, they spotted a solitary Roman legionary walking along a path. So they decided to ask _him_ the way out, Obelix lifting the poor man up by the scruff of his neck. The soldier immediately began to give directions but the only way they were going to make sense of them was by consulting a translator.

Does _OBELIX_ have a _TRANSLATOR_ with him? If so, use it to

work out the soldier's instruction by translating the content of his speech-balloon below. If he doesn't, go to 35 instead.

125

'Oh no, I was forgetting we didn't have any money with us,' said Asterix, and he started to apologise to the woman for bothering her. The woman said that she was very sorry she couldn't let them stay for nothing but her husband was off sick from work at the moment and she desperately needed the money. 'He's normally an aqueduct-builder,' she explained, 'but he's got a bad back at the moment and can't lift the stones.' Then Asterix had an idea. Instead of paying coins for their night's stay, they could give a magic potion. That would soon build up her husband's strength again!

Remove a MAGIC POTION CARD from ASTERIX'S WAIST-SLIT. Now go to 203.

126

Since Obelix didn't have a translator with him, they just had to guess what the Romans were saying. 'I think they're trying to tell us that we've got to go with them,' said Asterix, '. . . probably to become slaves or something.' Not very keen on this idea, they again tried to work free of their chains but it proved impossible, even for Obelix! Suddenly, though, he got an irritating little itch on his nose and, without thinking, he burst his chains apart so he could scratch it. 'Oh, I seem to have snapped them,' he said apologetically but, when he looked around for the Romans, he saw that they had fled! *Go to 16.*

127

Seeing that Obelix didn't have a translator, the Roman tried to explain, with sign language, why they had taken away his dog. 'I think he's saying that they don't want him messing up their nice clean pavements!' said Asterix after a while. Obelix immediately took offence at this, stomping right into the middle of the Romans, and Asterix thought he had better quickly take one of his magic potions so he could help him. 'Now who's messing up the pavements!' Obelix laughingly demanded a few minutes later as the stunned Romans lay all around them.

Remove a MAGIC POTION CARD from ASTERIX'S WAIST-SLIT. Now go to 39.

A few miles more and the Gauls arrived at the border with Germania. Asterix explained to Obelix that the Romans hadn't managed to invade Germania yet and the people there, the Goths, would probably give them a thorough questioning before letting them pass through. He proved to be absolutely right! 'Are you sure you're not Romans in disguise?' the Goth at the border post asked them. 'What is your business in Germania? Do you like our beer? . . .' Finally, though, he seemed to be convinced that they were friends of the Goths and he waved them over the frontier line.

Throw the special DICE to decide who is to cross the line first.

If you throw ASTERIX	go to 234
If you throw OBELIX	go to 195
If you throw DOGMATIX	go to 204

'That is correct – you may pass,' the soldiers told them when they had given *JULIUS* as the password. 'Welcome to the mighty country of Italia, land of the Romans!' They hadn't left the barrier far behind them when Asterix noticed that Obelix looked rather depressed. 'I always hate giving the right password,' his huge friend revealed to him sadly, staring at his feet. 'It means that we don't have an excuse for a fight!' *Go to 220.*

Suddenly sniffing the smell of leather, Dogmatix pointed his paw to a cobbler's shop on the far side of the square. While the Gauls were looking at the sandals in the rack outside, however, Asterix felt a firm tap on his shoulder. Turning round, he saw six huge Roman soldiers with a fat, spoilt-looking boy standing between them. As the youngster began to point a chubby finger at Dogmatix, one of the soldiers said something to them in Latin. 'I wonder what all this is about,' Asterix said, asking his friend to check if he had a translator.

If OBELIX does have a TRANSLATOR, use it to find out what the Roman was saying by translating the content of his speech-balloon below. If not, go to 269 instead.

'*HELMET* is correct,' the Roman captain told them with surprise. 'You may come ashore!' Wandering through the streets of Cosa, the Gauls came across a slave market. When the organiser spotted Obelix amongst the onlookers, however, he suddenly thought he would fetch a good price and so ordered his huge assistants to chain him. 'What am I bid for this large peasant?' the organiser asked as Obelix was brought forward. The bidding ended at a rather disappointing three-and-a-half coins, and Obelix was so offended that he broke his chains in two, wrapping them around the organiser's neck. 'Please, please, take this coinbag with all the day's profits,' the organiser begged as his face went a very funny colour!

If OBELIX doesn't already carry it, put the COINBAG into his WAIST-SLIT. Now go to 149.

132

They'd been following the Eporedia road for quite some time when they suddenly spotted some snow-capped mountains in the distance. 'Oh no, they're the Alps,' Asterix exclaimed. 'We've obviously been going in the wrong direction!' When they were at last heading in the *right* direction again, Asterix felt so weary that he drank one of his magic potions to revive his strength. 'Ah, that's better,' he said, stretching his arms. 'Now I feel I could walk all day!' Obelix and Dogmatix looked rather disgruntled at this, though, thinking it was all right for those with magic potions to help them!

Remove a MAGIC POTION CARD from ASTERIX'S WAIST-SLIT. Now go to 104.

'They're saying we can pass,' Obelix told his friend as he glanced over his translator. 'It looks like we *have* managed to take them in, after all!' So, desperately trying not to giggle and give it away, the Gauls continued down the steps as the guards opened a path for them. 'I always said these Romans were stupid,' Asterix remarked, with his sword still at Obelix's back. 'They not only don't find it odd that I'm a lot smaller than you, but they also don't seem to have noticed that I'm not even a Roman!' *Go to 87.*

They had passed quite a few milestones on the road to Vellaunodunum when Dogmatix's nose started twitching. 'I've seen that twitch before,' said Obelix excitedly, 'it means he can smell Romans!' And, sure enough, it wasn't long before they spotted a couple of Roman soldiers coming the other way. 'Look, what a puny-looking dog!' one of them laughed at Dogmatix. 'They're much fiercer-looking than that in Rome!' Obelix was absolutely incensed by the remark but Asterix held him back, insisting that Dogmatix should defend his honour himself. 'Please, down boy, down boy!' the Roman was soon imploring as Dogmatix repeatedly sank his teeth into his leg, and he offered the laughing Gauls a bag of coins to call Dogmatix off.

If OBELIX doesn't already carry it, put the COINBAG into his WAIST-SLIT. Now go to 154.

Journeying further and further into Helvetia, the Gauls eventually found themselves right amongst the mountains. 'Some of these would make very nice menhirs,' Obelix commented, glancing round. 'Perhaps I should take a couple back as souvenirs!' Asterix told him to leave the mountains alone, though, reminding him that they weren't there on holiday. Since it was growing dark, they started to look for a little guest-chalet in which to spend the night. It was only minutes after they had found one that they were fast asleep on the wooden beds, all that walking having tired them out!

Throw the special DICE to decide who is to be the first to awake in the morning.

If you throw ASTERIX   go to 264
If you throw OBELIX   go to 102
If you throw DOGMATIX   go to 227

They had gone some way along the Divodurum road, however, when they reached the border with Gaul again and so Asterix realised they must be going the wrong way. They turned back, choosing the road for Cambodunum this time. It took them through a large, black forest and the Gauls kept on the alert, knowing there were probably lots of bandits hiding inside. Suddenly, a dozen or so sprang out of the trees ahead and Asterix immediately drank one of his magic potions, ready to defend himself. In spite of the huge nailed clubs the bandits were armed with, they were soon all flattened on the ground. Obelix couldn't help feeling sorry for them, however, saying it was hardly surprising they were so weak when they only had those tiny little boars to feed on!

Remove a MAGIC POTION CARD from ASTERIX'S WAIST-SLIT. Now go to 157.

137

On the way to Vindonissa, however, they met a goatherd who told them that the Italian frontier was the other direction. 'And tell your little dog to stop bothering my goats,' he added irritably as Dogmatix scampered around them. 'It will spoil the flavour of their milk!' The Gauls at last reached the border with Italia and, seeing that it was heavily guarded by Romans, Asterix decided he had better take one of his magic potions. A few minutes later all the soldiers but one were knocked out cold. This one was just about still conscious, but had loads of stars before his eyes. 'W-w-welcome to Italia,' he said in a confused daze after the Gauls as they disappeared across the frontier!

Remove a MAGIC POTION CARD from ASTERIX'S WAIST-SLIT. Now go to 220. (Remember: when there are no magic potion cards left in Asterix's waist-slit their mission has to stop, and you must start the game again.)

The expression on the captain's face told Asterix that his guess at *ARMOUR* was wrong, and so he quickly drank one of his magic potions for the fight that was certain to occur. The cobbler's shop was soon completely devastated as the Romans went sailing into the shelves and the stacks of sandal boxes. As for the cobbler, he was knocked half-unconscious by a flying boot! 'Has Vesuvius erupted already?' he asked in a daze as he sat amongst all the wreckage. 'I thought it wasn't for another century or so!'

Remove a MAGIC POTION CARD from ASTERIX'S WAIST-SLIT. Now go to 79.

'Now this time make sure you don't say anything provocative!' Asterix warned his friend later, when they reached the gates of Aregenua. Fortunately, however, the sentry had dozed off in the hot sun and they were able to pass without trouble. 'We'll just get a few provisions for our journey,' Asterix said as they wandered through the mud streets, 'and then we'd better set off again.' The sentry was still asleep as they left, Dogmatix noticing that he had a bag of coins tucked into his belt. To teach him a lesson for not doing his job properly, Dogmatix very carefully pinched it from him!

If OBELIX doesn't already carry it, put the COINBAG into his waist-slit. Now go to 14.

140

'*JUPITER* is wrong,' the guard called back from behind the cell door. 'You must be trying to help the Druid escape!' And with that, he suddenly raised the alarm, bellowing as loudly as he could. 'Oh no, this looks like trouble!' Asterix remarked as they heard soldiers hurrying towards them from every quarter . . . *Go to 221.*

141

'He seems to be saying that we should follow this little path to the right,' Obelix remarked, continuing to hold the Roman's throat as he slowly read through his translator, '. . . and, apparently, that should take us to the road for Noviodunum,' he added, as he gave the soldier another shake. Obelix at last put the poor man down, the latter being so relieved that he even offered them a bag of coins to take on their travels.

If OBELIX doesn't already carry it, put the COINBAG into his WAIST-SLIT. Now go to 72.

'*JULIUS* is wrong!' the soldier exclaimed at the top of his voice. But just as he was about to order his guards to arrest Obelix (or, at least try and arrest him!), Asterix asked him whether it was Caesar's birthday today. 'Er . . . no,' the Roman replied, looking bewildered. Asterix then told him that was why Obelix had deliberately given the wrong password – because the right one should only be used on the proper day! The Roman was totally taken in by Asterix's cunning and even patted Obelix on the head for his show of respect! *Go to 66.*

Early next morning, the three friends were on their way again, soon reaching the town of Araines. Deciding they would like to have a rest from walking for a while, they searched round for a hay-cart station (the Gaulish equivalent of our bus station). At last they found one and, strolling round the platforms, they saw that there were three carts about to set off; one for Gennes, one for Vellaunodunum and one for Lutetia. Asterix asked his friend whether he had a map with him so they would know which was going in the direction they wanted.

If OBELIX does have a MAP with him, use it to find out which of

the three towns below is en route to Rome from Araines – then
follow the instruction. If he doesn't, you'll have to guess which
instruction to follow.

If you think it's GENNES   go to 218
If you think it's VELLAUNODUNUM   go to 4
If you think it's LUTETIA   go to 27

144

Since Obelix didn't have a translator, Asterix decided the only way they were going to find out the reason for their arrest was to accompany the Romans for a while. They could just have knocked them out there and then, of course, but Asterix was burning with curiosity! 'Ah, so that's it,' Asterix exclaimed as the Romans made them walk back to the striking slaves on the bridge. 'They think we belong with them and have escaped!' Now that his curiosity had been satisfied, he quickly drank one of his magic potions and then helped Obelix knock all the Romans into the water below. Not only did he force an apology from the Romans but he also made them promise to restore the slaves' overtime. 'And make sure that includes Sundays and Bank Holidays . . .' Flyingpicix insisted, becoming a bit greedy!

Remove a MAGIC POTION CARD from ASTERIX'S
WAIST-SLIT. Now go to 128.

Obelix reached the gangplank first, the other two not quite able to beat him. In truth, Asterix and Dogmatix *could* have beaten him to the raft but they both wanted to make sure it was safe enough. If it took Obelix's weight, then they knew it would take theirs as well! 'You two don't seem to be as fit as you used to be!' Obelix boasted innocently as they all sat down on a little wooden bench at the front. The raft was halfway across the lake when a ticket-man came up to them, saying that their total fare would be eight coins. Asterix had been in such a hurry to catch the raft that he had forgotten they would need some money. He only hoped Obelix had a coinbag with him!

If OBELIX does have a COINBAG, 'count out' the eight coins by rotating the disc – then go to the number that appears on the other side. If he doesn't, go to 187 instead.

Since Obelix didn't have a translator, Asterix decided they would just have to ignore what the Romans were trying to say and force their way through. So he immediately drank one of his magic potions and then helped Obelix despatch all of the soldiers through the air. They hadn't walked much further when they saw someone scooping up handfuls of snow from the mountain, stirring it into a pail of goat's milk. Asterix thought this rather strange but suddenly it all clicked. 'He's making ice-cream,' he exclaimed. 'And you know what that means – we're in Italia! So those Romans back there must have been guarding the frontier!'

Remove a MAGIC POTION CARD from ASTERIX'S WAIST-SLIT. Now go to 220. (Remember: when there are no magic potion cards left in Asterix's waist-slit their mission has to stop, and you must start the game again.)

147

The Gauls had just hidden themselves under the togas in the Eporedia cart when Asterix noticed that they seemed rather thicker than those in the Luca cart. 'That would suggest Eporedia isn't quite as warm,' he remarked thoughtfully, 'and so is probably further north!' Since it was *south* they needed to go for Rome, he therefore suggested they try the Luca cart instead! Asterix wasn't quite as clever as he liked to think, though, because, on the way to Luca, he suddenly noticed he was one gourd of magic potion short. He must have left it in the other cart!

Remove a MAGIC POTION CARD from ASTERIX'S WAIST-SLIT. Now go to 52.

148

Rather embarrassed by the situation, Asterix told the chalet-owner that they had forgotten they didn't have any money with them and they wouldn't be able to pay. So not only did they have to go without breakfast, but the owner made them clean out the chalet in return for last night's beds. Moreover, being Helvetian, he insisted that they do a thorough job of it! When they had finally finished, Asterix decided he had better drink one of his magic potions to restore his

strength. All that sweeping and scrubbing had been more tiring
than fighting a whole army of Romans. 'And much less fun!' Obelix
moaned wearily.

*Remove a **MAGIC POTION CARD** from **ASTERIX'S**
WAIST-SLIT. Now go to 84.*

149

After walking the whole of the day, the Gauls eventually reached the
town of Falerii, arriving there just before nightfall. Wandering
round, they soon found themselves a nice comfortable inn in which
to spend the night. The elderly innkeeper gave them a hearty supper
before showing them up to their rooms. Just as they were about to
get into bed, though, Asterix heard the innkeeper talking in Latin to
someone outside their room. Rather suspicious, he asked Obelix
if he had a translator so they could work out if the innkeeper was up
to something.

*If **OBELIX** does have a **TRANSLATOR**, use it to find out what
the innkeeper was saying by translating the content of his
speech-balloon below. If not, go to 199 instead.*

Creeping back out of the palace, the Gauls now hurriedly searched for the Colosseum. 'Look, there it is!' Asterix exclaimed, pointing to a huge stone stadium with lots of people queuing to get in. Reading down the programme of the afternoon's events plastered over the sides, they suddenly came to: 3 O'CLOCK – THE DRUID, GETAFIX, TO BE THROWN TO THE LIONS! 'We haven't got much time,' Asterix said. 'Quick, let's search for the entrance to the dungeons!' So they started to walk round the stadium, and eventually arrived at a heavy wooden door. Opening it, they saw that there was a flight of dark, dingy steps inside, leading downwards into the ground. 'This must be it!' Asterix exclaimed as they prepared to enter.

Throw the special DICE to decide who is to lead the way down the steps.

If you throw ASTERIX	go to 97
If you throw OBELIX	go to 172
If you throw DOGMATIX	go to 64

They finally agreed on Dogmatix's choice, following Obelix's little mongrel dog along the branch to the left. A milestone at the side of the road told them that they were on the way to the town of Alauna. Before they reached Alauna, however, the road met a wide river and the bridge that went across was full of Romans! Obelix was quite happy to go and fight their way through but Asterix thought it might be better to try and find another route across. 'Let's ask that fisherman down there,' he suggested, noticing a man with a rod a little further along, but the fisherman said that he would only direct them to an alternative crossing for four coins!

Does OBELIX have a COINBAG with him? If so, 'count out' four coins from the bag by rotating the disc until 4 shows in the window – then turn the card over to find out the fisherman's direction. If he doesn't have one, go to 173 instead.

They had walked quite a way in the direction of Alauna when Dogmatix's ears suddenly pricked up to a familiar sound in the distance. Moments later, Asterix and Obelix heard it too. 'There's only one person who sings as badly as that,' exclaimed Asterix, trying to block out the awful wail in his ears, 'it's Cacofonix, our local bard. We must be heading back towards our village!' So it was obvious that Alauna wasn't the right direction after all, and they made the long trek back to the signpost, deciding on the road for Araines this time. ***Go to 117.***

'The report tells how Getafix is being held in the strongest prison in Rome,' Obelix informed his friend as he slowly worked through his translator. 'And it says that, unless he reveals the secret of the magic potion by the end of the month, he will be thrown to the lions. Seat prices are thirty coins for the front rows and . . .' But Asterix suddenly tore the paper from him. 'We are not interested in what the seat prices are, you bird-brain,' he snapped. 'All we care about is how much time we've got!' He then glanced down, noticing that something had fluttered from the paper to the floor. 'Look, it's a password scroll,' he commented, picking it up. 'Some Roman must have left it in his paper by mistake!'

If OBELIX doesn't already carry it, put the PASSWORD SCROLL into his WAIST-SLIT. Now go to 143.

The days went rapidly by and, by the time our Gaulish heroes had reached the town of Alesia, they had been travelling for a whole week. 'Let's go and see if we can find some roast boar,' Obelix suggested hungrily after knocking out the sentry at the gate. 'They're bound to have some in a town of this size!' Sure enough, they soon spotted a likely-looking place, 'The Boar's Ears', and they hurried up to it.

Throw the special DICE to decide who is to reach the inn first.

If you throw ASTERIX   go to 257

If you throw OBELIX   go to 58

If you throw DOGMATIX   go to 245

Scanning his translator, Obelix told his friend that the Romans were accusing them of being escaped slaves and were going to take them back to join the other slaves on the bridge. 'Oh, are they?' Asterix exclaimed and he drew out his sword, about to cut them all down to size. But then he suddenly changed his mind, weakly dropping his sword to the ground as if it was too heavy for him. Obelix couldn't understand what he was doing . . . until the Romans all walked away, tutting at them as they went. His cunning little friend had made them think they were so feeble that they weren't worth having as slaves! *Go to 111.*

The Bergomum road twisted higher and higher, going right up into the mountains. 'Well, at least it's nice to find a Roman road that isn't straight for a change!' said Obelix as they panted away. They had now reached the snowline and the road became little more than a narrow track. Just as this track was running along the edge of a steep precipice, they spotted a patrol of Romans coming the other way. Since there wasn't room for both of them, the Gauls decided that they would just have to knock them over the edge! 'Have a nice Swiss roll, won't you?' Obelix chuckled as they watched the Romans tumble over and over in the snow beneath them. One of the soldiers had dropped a coinbag during the fight and Dogmatix now picked it up, handing it to his master.

If OBELIX doesn't already carry it, put the COINBAG into his WAIST-SLIT. Now go to 20.

The three travellers finally left Germania, crossing the border into a country called Noricum (the Roman name for Austria). It was a very mountainous land and all the people seemed to be bards, singing and writing down music! 'It's a pity we couldn't bring Cacofonix here to learn a few lessons!' Asterix remarked as the beautiful voices and lyre-playing echoed round the valleys. It wasn't many miles before they came to a large mountain pass and they were about halfway along when they were stopped by a line of Romans. They started to shout something in Latin in chorus and so Asterix asked his friend if he had a translator with him.

If OBELIX does have a TRANSLATOR, use it to find out what the Romans were saying by translating the speech-balloon below. If he doesn't, go to 146 instead.

158

'Asterix . . . Obelix!' the Druid exclaimed with joy when he saw who it was. 'What a timely arrival!' As Dogmatix licked the old Druid's face, Asterix asked him whether his captivity had been too much of an ordeal. 'Oh, not at all,' Getafix replied. 'In fact, I've quite enjoyed teasing these Romans. Every time they thought they were just about to get the ingredients for the magic potion out of me, I pretended I had forgotten it!' When Asterix had finished laughing at this, he said they had better get moving before the whole of the Roman army arrived on the scene. So he led the way back up the dungeon steps and out into the open air again. They then left Rome, hurriedly following the road to the nearest port. Luckily, they found a merchant galley just about to set sail for northern Gaul . . . and, after a journey considerably more relaxing than the outward one, they at last reached their little village! 'Tonight we'll have a massive banquet to celebrate,' the chief announced jubilantly on seeing that Asterix's mission had been successful. 'And tomorrow, Getafix, you can start mixing some more of your magic potions – for our *next* fight with the Romans!'

You have successfully completed the game. Well done!

159

As soon as the two Gauls gave the password as *SWORD* the man's face completely changed. '*SWORD* is correct,' he said hugging them to his breast. 'Welcome – fellow enemies of Rome!' When Asterix told the man his name he became even more cordial. 'So you're the famous Asterix,' he exclaimed with admiration as he showed them to the best sleeping-quarters he had. 'We've often heard of your great courage!' Feeling a bit left out, Obelix asked the man if he had heard of his courage too. 'Yes, of course, *Dogmatix*,' the man replied, slapping him on the shoulder. 'It's well known that you're Asterix's trusty friend!' ***Go to 203.***

160

The Gauls had only been on the Falerii road for a few minutes when they saw a finely-dressed Roman on a horse coming the other way. 'Out of my path, pigs!' he ordered them. 'My name is Pompus and I'm one of Caesar's most important officials!' Obelix immediately lost his temper at this – not because he was insulted, but because the mention of pigs made him feel hungry! 'Don't you have any tact?' he demanded as he pulled the Roman from his horse and tossed him into the ditch. 'I haven't eaten for hours!' As they continued on their journey again, Asterix noticed that Dogmatix was carrying a password scroll in his mouth. It must have dropped from the Roman's belt!

If OBELIX doesn't already carry it, put the PASSWORD SCROLL into his WAIST-SLIT. Now go to 45.

161

'Yes, they *are* letting us past!' Obelix said as, reading through his translator, he found out that the guards were telling them to report to the head cook inside the palace. They had only gone a few steps further, however, when one of the guards became suspicious, saying that he had never heard of the palace employing Gaulish cooks before. Obelix suddenly swung round and grabbed him by the throat, demanding what was wrong with Gaulish cooks. 'Gaulish cooking is famed throughout the world,' he told him passionately. 'No one can do sauces like we can!' The guard was so petrified of this big hulk that he offered Obelix a bag of coins to put him down again.

If OBELIX doesn't already carry it, put the COINBAG into his WAIST-SLIT. Now go to 34.

162

The three travellers didn't have to follow Asterix's choice of road far before they spotted a small town in the distance. 'That must be the Roman-occupied town of Noviodunum,' said Asterix. 'Let's see if we can sneak in through the town gates and get some more information about Getafix's kidnapping.' They noticed a large hay-cart heading for the town and they decided to walk on the blind side of that. Just as they were about to pass the centurion at the gates, however, he lowered his pike at them and insisted on knowing the town password. 'We don't want anyone fishy coming into Novio-dunum,' he said. 'So, either give me the correct password or you'll catch this pike!'

Does OBELIX have a PASSWORD SCROLL on him? If so,

use it to find out the correct password by placing exactly over the scroll shape below – then follow the appropriate instruction. If he doesn't have one, you'll have to guess which instruction to follow.

If you think it's JUPITER	go to 182
If you think it's MERCURY	go to 98
If you think it's NEPTUNE	go to 224

TIBERIUS was obviously incorrect because the door was immediately slammed shut. When Obelix arrived, he suggested that they just force their way in but then Asterix noticed an old pig-sty at the back. 'Let's go and sleep in there,' he suggested, feeling a bit too tired for a fight. 'It looks perfectly dry and I much prefer the smell of swine to that of Romans anyway!' ***Go to 143.***

164

'They're saying that they are ruthless bandits from Corsica . . .' Obelix calmly explained as he scanned his translator, '. . . and they want every possession we've got!' Obelix then started to use the translator to give the bandits his reply but he soon decided there was a much quicker way of replying. 'Here, this should be a lot easier to understand!' he said as, one by one, he knocked them to the ground. Yapping amongst all the dazed bodies, Dogmatix suddenly picked up a map. 'Look, it's a map of the Roman Empire,' exclaimed Asterix. 'It must have fallen from one of their pockets!'

If OBELIX doesn't already carry it, put the MAP into his WAIST-SLIT. Now go to 154.

165

The Gauls hadn't gone far on the Avaricum road when they were ordered to turn back by a Roman on horseback. He said there had been a multiple chariot pile-up a little further along and they would have to try some other route. So they took the road for Valentia but, again, they hadn't gone far before their journey was interrupted. A patrol of Romans told them that they were looking for some slaves

for Caesar to send as a gift to Cleopatra and that Obelix was just the sort of person they wanted. When they tried to put some chains on Obelix, however, the two Gauls sprang into action, scattering the Romans all across the road. 'That's the second pile-up today!' Asterix laughed as he drank one of his magic potions to restore his strength.

Remove a MAGIC POTION CARD from ASTERIX'S WAIST-SLIT. Now go to 111.

166

'*EAGLE* is incorrect,' the Romans told them with a snigger. 'I'm afraid you'll just have to walk all the way round the gorge!' But Obelix suddenly grabbed two Romans by the throat, one in each hand, and dangled them over the edge. 'No, what we meant was – you're quite welcome to use our rope-car!' the Romans stammered as he threatened to drop them. So the Gauls stepped into the little wooden cabin, immediately being ferried across to the opposite mountain. 'You know, those Romans can be quite helpful if you ask them nicely!' Obelix chuckled. *Go to 84.*

167

The galley carrying our heroes was just passing the Gaulish port of Antipolis when a small fire broke out on board. The galley therefore quickly made for the harbour and the three Gauls found themselves on land again. Luckily, though, they saw that there were three other galleys about to leave from Antipolis. One was sailing for Massilia, one for Narbo and one for Albingaunum. Asterix asked his friend if he had a map so they would know which of these ports was in the direction they wanted. Otherwise, they would just have to take pot luck!

If OBELIX does have a MAP with him, use it to find out which of the three ports below is in the right direction for Rome from Antipolis – then follow the appropriate instruction. If he doesn't, you'll have to guess which instruction to follow.

If you think it's MASSILIA	go to 103
If you think it's NARBO	go to 7
If you think it's ALBINGAUNUM	go to 120

The Romans immediately drew out their swords, telling them that *LION* was wrong. Their leader said that they would give them one last chance, however, asking the innkeeper to bring out another Italian dish to see if they could identify that. 'Of course we can,' Obelix remarked when a large bowl of spaghetti arrived, 'it's boiled worms!' Asterix clapped his hand to his head (and Dogmatix his paw!) in despair as Obelix went on to say how he thought boiling

worms was rather cruel. 'I think it's magic potion time . . .' the little
Gaul sighed to himself and he quickly uncorked one of the gourds.
Soon after, the Romans were all heaped on top of each other, the
spaghetti slithering down their faces. 'Oh, I do feel sorry for them,'
Obelix remarked as he cleaned his hands. 'First they're boiled and
put in a bowl and now they're stuck to those horrible Romans!'

**Remove a MAGIC POTION CARD from ASTERIX'S
WAIST-SLIT. Now go to 21.**

169

'What a cheek!' Obelix remarked when he had opened his
translator. 'He's telling us to remove our helmets so that he can see!'
Obelix's favourite game, though, was removing *Romans'* helmets
(generally, after knocking them out!) and he didn't see why this one
should be any exception. So he reached up to grab the officer's
helmet, which dropped to the ground. In fact, his helmet wasn't the
only thing that dropped to the ground. For, lying next to it, was a
large map of the Roman Empire!

**If OBELIX doesn't already carry it, put the MAP into his
WAIST-SLIT. Now go to 104.**

On their way to Falerii, Dogmatix sniffed out a long, tubular thing at the side of the road. Assuming it to be a boar bone, his master's face lit up. If there were boar bones round there, it was a logical deduction that there should also be boars! When Asterix had a closer look at the object, however, he had to disappoint his friend. It wasn't a bone at all but a password scroll!

If OBELIX doesn't already have it, put the PASSWORD SCROLL into his WAIST-SLIT. Now go to 149.

171

They had been following the road for Noviodunum for quite some time when Dogmatix spotted a milestone in the grass. 'Oh no,' exclaimed Asterix, clapping his hand to his brow, 'it says that Noviodunum is another fifty-three miles! It looks as if it wasn't the nearest town to Alauna after all!' So they made their long way back again, deciding on the road for Aregenua this time. 'Of course, if the Romans weren't so stingy with their milestones,' Asterix commented grumpily as they at last approached Aregenua, 'we wouldn't have wasted all this time. I've a good mind to complain!'
Go to 81.

Obelix had led them halfway down the steps when their path was suddenly blocked by about a dozen Roman guards. 'Shall we hit them?' Obelix asked his friend eagerly, but Asterix said they would first of all try tricking their way past. So he pointed his sword at Obelix's back, pretending that he was bringing another prisoner to the dungeons. He couldn't be sure whether the Romans were taken in by this or not, though, because, when one of them made some sort of comment, it was in Latin!

Does OBELIX have a TRANSLATOR with him? If so, use it to find out what the Roman was saying by translating the content of his speech-balloon below. If not, go to 13 instead.

SUT LIM IGI HOS TUL EBBA ILO

Asterix told the fisherman that they didn't have four coins, though, and even if they did it would be daylight robbery! So it looked as if they were just going to have to fight their way through those Romans after all. Obelix was barely able to keep the grin off his face! One by one, the Romans were sent flying off the bridge into the water below, and the Gauls were eventually able to proceed to the other side. 'You would think they would take some of their clothes off before going for a swim, wouldn't you?' Obelix chuckled as they continued towards Alauna. ***Go to 55.***

174

'Getafix must have been taken to that town because there was a good strong prison there,' Asterix told his friend as they waited for their drinks. The drinks at last arrived and Obelix uncorked the huge barrel of beer he had ordered. He glugged it down in one, looking a little disappointed when the barrel was empty. 'They serve such small measures in here!' he remarked. 'Still, I suppose I shouldn't complain since it was free!' ***Go to 66.***

175

In spite of the fact that he was the heaviest, Obelix reached the inn first. He had suddenly smelt roast boar coming from the place and it made him make a special effort! It wasn't long before they were all sitting down to that roast boar but their meal was interrupted by a loud knock at the door. 'This is an armed patrol,' shouted a Roman voice. 'We're searching everywhere for wanted Gauls – so open up!' Being a rather greedy man, the innkeeper whispered to Asterix that he would only hide them for twenty coins.

Does OBELIX have a COINBAG with him? If so 'count out' the twenty coins for the innkeeper by rotating the disc – then go to the number that appears on the other side. If he doesn't, go to 256 instead.

'Oh, goody,' Obelix exclaimed when the Goths told them that *DAGGER* was wrong, 'does that mean you're going to feed us that delicious cream cake now?' Asterix said that he didn't think that was quite what they meant by forcing it down their throats, though, and hurriedly drank one of his magic potions. The Goths were soon strewn across the inn floor and the Gauls returned to their meal. 'I wonder what this black bread is called?' Obelix asked casually as he munched on a slice of pumpernickel, but Asterix quickly told him to shut up!

Remove a *MAGIC POTION CARD* from *ASTERIX'S WAIST-SLIT*. Now go to 157.

'He seems to like it!' Obelix exclaimed after his little dog had nibbled a bit of his pizza. 'In fact, he looks nearly as happy as when he's eating boar bones!' But just as Obelix was about to bite into the pizza himself, his friend suddenly spotted a large company of Romans through the window. 'They're coming towards the inn,' Asterix said urgently. 'Quick, we'd better think of something before they arrive!' They were still wondering what to do when the innkeeper told them that he had two Roman uniforms in his possession, left by a couple of soldiers who had become so drunk one evening that they had walked out in their underwear! 'But it's a big risk I'm taking,' the innkeeper added greedily. 'So it will cost you sixteen coins!'

Does OBELIX have a COINBAG with him? If so, 'count out' the sixteen coins by rotating the disc, then go to the number that appears on the other side. If not, go to 213 instead.

178

'We'll just have to pretend we've got water in our ears and haven't heard him, then!' Asterix remarked when Obelix said he didn't have a translator. But the Roman attendant began shouting for assistance and there were suddenly soldiers all round the edge of the bath. Dogmatix immediately pulled himself out and then ran and fetched one of Asterix's magic potions from his clothes. 'Thanks, just what I need!' Asterix said as he drank it in one. Five minutes later, the Gauls were calmly getting dressed again . . . and the poor Romans, of course, were floundering and spluttering in the water!

Remove a MAGIC POTION CARD from ASTERIX'S WAIST-SLIT. Now go to 52.

179

Obelix said he didn't have any coins on him, however, and so the old man refused to help them, scurrying off. 'Not very friendly here, are they?' exclaimed Asterix as they began to search for another inn themselves. Again, it was Dogmatix's nose that did the trick, guiding them towards a cosy little place on the other side of town. 'That nose of his knows what it's doing!' Obelix chuckled to his friend proudly as they followed the little dog through the inn door. *Go to 108.*

180

The other two followed behind Obelix as he led the way up to the huge stone gateway. He was intending just to knock the guards out but Asterix told him to hold on for a while, seeing if they could trick their way past first. 'We don't want to attract the attention of the rest of the palace guard,' he told him. 'And, besides, I might well need my magic potions for later!' So, when they reached the guards, the little Gaul told them they were new cooks for the palace kitchens. The guards' reply came in Latin, however, and without a translator the Gauls couldn't be sure whether they were letting them through or not!

Does OBELIX have a TRANSLATOR with him? If so, use it to find out what the guards were saying by translating the content of the speech-balloon below. If not, go to 216 instead.

'*NEPTUNE* is correct,' the guard replied, and he slowly began to open the cell door for them. As soon as it was wide enough, the Gauls burst in, knocking the guard out! They looked round the cell for Getafix, suddenly spotting him in the corner . . . *Go to 158.*

'*JUPITER* is wrong!' the centurion said with delight, about to raise the alarm. But Asterix just managed to stop him, pressing a hand against his mouth. 'I didn't say it *was* the password,' he lied with a wink at Obelix. 'What I said was "By Jupiter!" '– not believing that such well-known townspeople as us should have to bother with this nonsense. I know you've got a pike in your hand but that doesn't mean you have to be so o-fish-ous!' The centurion was so belittled by this remark that he immediately removed his pike, ushering them through. *Go to 72.*

'I've found one!' said Obelix delightedly, lumbering up to where a B and B sign hung from a hut door. When they knocked on the door, however, they were confronted by a man with a rather hostile-looking face. 'This place is only open to enemies of Rome,' he said. 'Prove yourself by giving the right password!'

Does OBELIX have a PASSWORD SCROLL with him? If

so, use it to find out the correct password by placing exactly over the scroll shape below – then follow the appropriate instruction. If he doesn't have one, you'll have to guess which instruction to follow.

If you think it's SWORD   go to 159
If you think it's JAVELIN   go to 243
If you think it's DAGGER   go to 88

SWORD was clearly the wrong password, however, because, as soon as they had uttered it, the sentry shouted for assistance. 'Right, you're to be taken to Rome where you'll be thrown to the lions!' he told them when the others had arrived. Obelix said that his little dog might be frightened by the lions, though, and so he didn't want to go. 'What do you mean, you don't want to go?' the Roman asked, rather taken aback. So our Gaulish heroes began to explain to them— with their fists! It wasn't long before the Romans were all flattened on the ground and Asterix drank one of his magic potions to rebuild his strength for the next encounter.

*Remove a **MAGIC POTION CARD** from **ASTERIX'S WAIST-SLIT**. Now go to 154.* (Remember: when there are no magic potion cards left in Asterix's waist-slit their mission has to stop, and you must start the game again from the beginning.)

185

No sooner had Obelix said that he didn't have nine coins than the soothsayer shouted for a detachment of Romans at the back of the inn. He told the Gauls that he was really an agent in disguise and they were to be arrested for going on a mission against Rome. 'You and your big mouth!' Asterix remarked to his friend with a sigh as he quickly drank one of his magic potions. As soon as they had dealt with all the Romans, the Gauls then turned on the soothsayer. 'I foresee that you're going to have quite a headache in the morning!' Asterix chuckled, as they were about to knock him across the room.

*Remove a **MAGIC POTION CARD** from **ASTERIX'S WAIST-SLIT**. Now go to 39.*

Obelix swam to the other side of the river first, nearly emptying it with his frantic arm movements! 'Hey, do you mind?' the slaves shouted at him from the bridge. 'You've made us all soaking wet!' After drying off in the sun, the Gauls continued on their way but they hadn't gone far when they were arrested by a patrol of Romans. Asterix insisted on knowing the reason for their arrest but the Romans only seemed to be able to speak in Latin. 'I wonder what they're trying to tell us,' Asterix pondered as he asked Obelix if he had a translator.

If OBELIX does have a TRANSLATOR, use it to find what the Romans were saying by translating the content of the speech-balloon below. If he doesn't, go to 144 instead.

Unfortunately, Obelix *didn't* have a coinbag with him and the ticket-man said they would have to choose between being thrown overboard or being handed over to the Roman garrison at the other side. By the time Obelix had come to a decision, however, the raft was only a couple of metres from the shore. 'I think I'd prefer being

handed over to the Romans,' he said. 'I'm worried that Dogmatix might catch a bit of a chill in that water!' So Asterix quickly drank one of his magic potions, ready for the punch-up that was bound to occur. '. . . On thinking about it, though,' Obelix commented a little later when they had knocked the whole of the garrison out, 'maybe Dogmatix would have enjoyed a little swim!'

*Remove a **MAGIC POTION CARD** from **ASTERIX'S WAIST-SLIT**. Now go to 20.*

188

'Right, prepare yourself for the lions!' the Roman barked as their guess at *WOLF* proved wrong. Obelix shook all his captors off, though, saying that he'd never had a meal of lions before and wasn't sure he would like them. 'Now, if I was preparing myself for a meal of boar, that would be totally different!' he added eagerly. Asterix could see the Romans growing more and more angry and so he decided it was time to make a dash for it. 'But they might have been about to offer us boar!' Obelix protested as his little friend dragged him through all the spectators and out into the safety of the streets. *Go to 104.*

189

Obelix leapt into his hammock first, nearly stretching it to the floor as it strained under his weight! Rather more elegantly, the other two got into their hammocks as well and it wasn't long before they were all sound asleep. Before they knew it, it was morning again and the three friends stood watching on the deck as the galley entered Cosa harbour. They were just about to step ashore, however, when the owner of the galley tactfully reminded them that they hadn't paid for the trip yet. 'Let me see now,' he said, totting up on his fingers. 'Two humans and a dog – one way – with hammocks . . . that will be ten coins please!'

Does OBELIX have a COINBAG with him? If so, 'count out' the ten coins by rotating the disc – then go to the number that appears on the other side. If he doesn't, go to 86 instead.

190

Although the Gauls didn't have a translator, they were soon able to guess what the Romans had been announcing. For they started moving round the breakfast tables, forcing money out of everyone. They had obviously been announcing that they were tax-collectors! The Romans had now come to the chalet-owner and, since he had been such a friendly host, the Gauls decided it was time for them to act. Asterix quickly mixed one of his magic potions into his muesli and then joined Obelix in hurling the petrified Romans through the window. 'See, I told you that muesli was very healthy for you!' the chalet-owner told them gratefully.

Remove a MAGIC POTION CARD from ASTERIX'S WAIST-SLIT. Now go to 84.

'Right, arrest these men,' one of the Romans ordered to the others. '*HELMET* is wrong – and so they can't be doctors after all!' While they were trying to pin his hands behind his back, Obelix couldn't help giggling. 'Of course we're not doctors,' he tittered. 'When have you ever seen doctors with swords sticking out of their belts?' He was still chuckling away while Asterix quickly drank one of his magic potions – and then knocked all the Romans down the steps! 'Where did they all go?' Obelix asked bewilderedly when he could finally control himself.

Remove a MAGIC POTION CARD from ASTERIX'S WAIST-SLIT. Now go to 107. (Remember: when there are no magic potion cards left in Asterix's waist-slit their mission is over, and you must start the game again.)

Asterix was left with the shortest blade of grass himself and so he scratched his head, trying to think up a clever distraction. 'I know!' he exclaimed suddenly, and promptly marched up to the town gates. 'Excuse me,' he said to the rather simple-looking guard, 'but you've got purple spots all over your face. You don't think it could be this new plague that's going round, do you?' But the trick didn't work quite as he had hoped. 'No, that brings you out in orange spots,' the guard replied vacantly. 'Now, give me the password or I can't let you enter.' A little deflated, Asterix plodded back to his two friends, asking Obelix if he had a password scroll with him!

*Does **OBELIX** have a **PASSWORD SCROLL** with him? If he does, use it to find out the correct password by placing exactly over the scroll shape below – then follow the appropriate instruction. If he doesn't, you'll have to guess which instruction to follow.*

If you think it's **JUPITER**   go to 63
If you think it's **MERCURY**   go to 271
If you think it's **NEPTUNE**   go to 249

193

'She's telling us that she's Hispanic,' Obelix said as he quickly consulted his translator, 'but she's settled in Gaul because she couldn't stand the sight of all that bull-fighting!' But Asterix told him not to mind about the gossip, just to ask whether she had any vacancies for the night. Obelix began to put the words together but it took him so long that Dogmatix fell asleep on the doorstep. 'Never mind, never mind,' Asterix told his friend as he still tried to persevere with the question. 'Look, she's inviting us in anyway. Dogmatix obviously has much simpler ways of making himself understood!' *Go to 203.*

194

'I think *SWORD* must have been wrong!' Asterix whispered to his friend as the waiter's face filled with rage. 'Yes, I think you're probably right!' Obelix whispered back as all the other customers started to close in on them. Asterix quickly drank one of his magic potions ready for the confrontation but he was rather reluctant to fight his fellow Gauls. So he decided just to scare them off instead, using his suddenly-increased strength to lift Obelix on to his shoulder. The idea worked, for all the customers immediately moved aside, allowing him a path towards the door. 'It didn't make *me* look very strong, though, did it!' Obelix complained when his friend had put him down again on the other side.

*Remove a **MAGIC POTION CARD** from **ASTERIX'S WAIST-SLIT**. Now go to 67.*

Obelix crossed into Germania first, his two friends right behind him. The road they followed into the next town was very wide and full of fast chariots. 'By Jupiter, we were lucky not to have been run down then!' Asterix exclaimed angrily as one brushed right past them at full gallop. Yet another chariot went by but this one, with blue candles on the horses' heads, suddenly stopped right in front of them. The uniformed Goth at the reins told them that this was a chariotway (the ancient predecessor of the modern motorway!) and was for the use of chariots only. He said that the fine for any pedestrians using it was five coins and, if they didn't pay up, he would have to take them to gaol!

Does OBELIX carry a COINBAG with him? If so, use it to 'count out' these five coins by rotating the disc – then go to the number that appears on the other side. If not, go to 112 instead.

'No, *AUGUSTUS* is wrong – you must be invaders!' the Romans said, and the Gauls suddenly found themselves being arrested. Asterix first tried to argue their way out of the situation, saying that an invader would hardly be as small as himself and bring a dog with him. But, when that didn't work, he decided he would just have to drink one of his magic potions. A brief fight later, the Gauls were calmly stepping into Italia. 'I always find it a little sad when violence is the only thing that has any effect!' Asterix chuckled as they picked their way amongst all the groaning bodies.

Remove a MAGIC POTION CARD from ASTERIX'S WAIST-SLIT. Now go to 220. (Remember: when there are no magic potion cards left in Asterix's waist-slit their mission has to stop, and you must start the game again.)

197

'You're saying that we're peasants . . . scum . . . pigs!' Obelix told the Roman as he peeped at his translator. In fact, Obelix was so delighted at being able to fool him like this that it took a while for the Roman's words to sink in! When they did, Obelix suddenly swept him off the ground by his throat. 'It was just a test – a test!' the terrified Roman pleaded and he offered Obelix a password scroll to show that he didn't mean any of it.

If OBELIX doesn't already carry it, put the PASSWORD SCROLL into his WAIST-SLIT. Now go to 21.

198

'So you're spies, then!' the Romans exclaimed as *MERCURY* proved incorrect. They said that they could choose between being thrown into the sea or doing thirty years' hard labour working the oars in the bottom of their galley. 'Will we be given regular snacks while we're rowing?' Obelix asked, trying to make his decision – but Asterix was already drinking one of his magic potions. A couple of thuds, a clonk and the odd blam or two later, and the Romans were all spluttering in the sea. 'Oh, I also wanted to ask them if I'd be allowed to take Dogmatix with me!' Obelix tutted at his friend's impatience.

Remove a MAGIC POTION CARD from ASTERIX'S WAIST-SLIT. Now go to 167.

199

'Oh well, perhaps what he's saying is all perfectly innocent,' Asterix remarked when Obelix told him that he didn't have a translator. A moment later, though, their door burst open and in rushed the innkeeper with about a dozen soldiers. The innkeeper had obviously suspected who they were! Quickly drinking one of his magic potions, Asterix was soon joining Obelix in taking the soldiers on. When all the soldiers were knocked out, the Gauls then turned their attention to the innkeeper, tying him up so he wouldn't cause any more trouble. 'Are you sure we aren't being a bit rash?' Obelix asked as they then bundled the old man into a cupboard. 'Now there won't be anyone to cook our breakfast in the morning!'

Remove a MAGIC POTION CARD from ASTERIX'S WAIST-SLIT. Now go to 45. (Remember: when there are no magic potion cards left in Asterix's waist-slit their mission has to stop, and you must start the game again.)

'*TIBERIUS* is right,' one of the guards told them with a little embarrassment. He added that he was sorry he hadn't believed them but Asterix looked much too small to be a bodyguard. 'Well, how come I didn't look too small to be an assassin, then?' Asterix snapped. The guards tried to explain how an assassin needn't be quite as big as a bodyguard but they got themselves so confused that they just waved the Gauls past. 'I always said those Romans were crazy!' Asterix remarked with a secret chuckle as they approached the palace doors. *Go to 34.*

It was Dogmatix who spotted an inn first. Well, not so much spotted it as smelt it – his nose leading him to where the smell of wild boar pie came wafting from a window! But when the two Gauls poked their heads round the inn door, they saw that it was full of Romans. 'We'd better look for somewhere else,' whispered Asterix, 'I'd never trust the food in a place that the Romans liked!' Just at that moment, a rather bedraggled-looking old man tapped them on the shoulder, saying that he would lead them to the best inn in town. But it would cost them seven coins for his services!

Does OBELIX have a COINBAG with which to pay? If so, 'count out' seven coins from the bag by rotating the disc until 7 shows in the window – then turn the card over to find out the old man's instructions. If he doesn't have one, go to 179 instead.

'Oh, I forgot we didn't have any money on us,' said Obelix, going a little red. 'Perhaps we should offer to do the washing-up instead!' But the tavern-owner angrily told them that he could do his own washing-up, saying that it was bad enough that the Romans always came to eat there for nothing. Then Asterix thought of a way he could help. 'We'll pay for our breakfast with this,' he told him, handing him one of his gourds of magic potion. 'All you have to do is take a few drops each morning and then the Romans won't dare to refuse to pay!'

Remove a MAGIC POTION CARD from ASTERIX'S WAIST-SLIT. Now go to 16.

After a good night's sleep, our three travellers arose eager and refreshed the next morning. Leaving Araines, they saw there was a choice of three roads they could follow. The first led to the town of Gennes, the second to the town of Lutetia and the third to the town of Vellaunodunum. 'I wonder which one we should take?' asked Asterix, removing his helmet to scratch his head. Obelix started feeling through his huge pockets to see if he had a map with him.

If OBELIX does have a MAP, use it to find which of the three towns is in the best direction for Rome from Araines – then follow the instruction. If he doesn't, you'll have to guess which instruction to follow.

If you think GENNES	go to 110
If you think LUTETIA	go to 38
If you think VELLAUNODUNUM	go to 134

Trotting just in front of his master, it was Dogmatix who crossed the frontier line first. This part of Germania seemed to consist of a huge forest but their road eventually led to a clearing with a small town in it. All feeling very hungry, they found themselves an inn. Instead of getting boar as they were hoping for, though, they were brought a

large dark cake decorated with cherries and whipped goat's cream.
Obelix asked the innkeeper what it was called and he told them
it was a Black Forest cake, and that it was a speciality of the area.
Overhearing this conversation, a dozen or so Goth warriors from the
next table said that if they didn't know what the cake was called,
they must be Roman spies! 'Tell us what the local password is,' they
demanded, drawing their swords, 'or we'll force that cake right
down your throats!'

*Does OBELIX have a PASSWORD SCROLL with him? If so,
use it to find out the correct password by placing exactly over the
scroll shape below – then follow the appropriate instruction. If he
doesn't have one, you'll have to guess which instruction to
follow.*

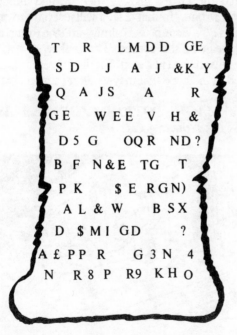

If you think it's SWORD	go to 105
If you think it's JAVELIN	go to 266
If you think it's DAGGER	go to 176

205

'No, you can't have another guess at the password!' the leader of the Romans told the Gauls angrily when he had announced that *EAGLE* was wrong. 'In that case, it will just have to be one of my magic potions . . .' Asterix said calmly – and the Romans were soon a mangled heap in the corner. The innkeeper was absolutely stunned by what he had just seen, offering the Gauls as many pizzas as they liked in the hope that they wouldn't suspect his treachery!

Remove a *MAGIC POTION CARD* from *ASTERIX'S WAIST-SLIT*. Now to go 21.

206

Seeing that their guess at *ARMOUR* was wrong, the Gauls decided to make a run for it, dashing into the town. The Romans were close behind them and so, as soon as they had turned a corner, Asterix told his friends to freeze as if they were statues. There were so many statues in the town that it was only when they had gone a long way past that the Romans realised there was something odd about these ones. Two statues in bright clothes – and a dog! By the time the Romans had returned, though, the Gauls were in a totally different part of the town. The only misfortune for our heroes during the chase was that Asterix had dropped one of his magic potions!

Remove a *MAGIC POTION CARD* from *ASTERIX'S WAIST-SLIT*. Now go to 149.

207

Dogmatix couldn't be bothered with silly discussions, though, just leading the way up to the palace gates himself! As they followed the little dog, Asterix told Obelix to pretend to the guards that they were decorators appointed to paint one of the rooms. The guards immediately barred their way, however, telling them that they couldn't enter. But it wasn't because they didn't believe them, as Asterix feared . . . it was simply that they wouldn't allow dogs in the palace grounds! The Gauls were just thinking that they would have to knock them out when one of the guards whispered something in Asterix's ear. 'I'll tell you what we'll do,' he said, corruptly. 'Slip us three coins and we'll pretend we haven't seen the dog!'

Does OBELIX have a COINBAG with him? If so, 'count out' the three coins by rotating the disc – then go to the number that appears on the other side. If not, go to 231 instead.

It was Asterix who spotted a B and B sign first, pointing to a cosy little hut with a chimney smoking away. As he knocked on the door, he now told the others what the letters stood for. 'The first B is for bed,' he said with a broad grin, 'and the second B is for breakfast. There isn't a B for boar and there isn't one for bone either!' Obelix didn't mind that much, though, because he thought there was a good chance the breakfast could be boar. And of course Dogmatix thought there was a good chance it could be bone! Asterix was just about to knock on the door again when a plump woman answered, saying that a night would cost them eighteen coins.

Does OBELIX carry a COINBAG? If so, 'count out' eighteen coins by rotating the disc – and then go to the number that shows on the other side. If not, go to 125 instead.

'Yes, *TIBERIUS* is correct,' the Roman replied sternly, 'you may continue with your drinking, barbarian.' Obelix was wondering whether to demand an apology from the stupid man . . . knowing that it would lead to a fight! But it might result in a lot of damage to the inn and so he decided to resist. He wanted some way of cheeking the stuck-up Roman, though, and so he pinched a document sticking out from his leather belt as he passed. Opening it up after the patrol had left, he saw that it was a map of the Roman Empire!

If OBELIX doesn't already carry it, put the MAP into his WAIST-SLIT. Now go to 66.

210

On the road to Valentia, the Gauls came across an exhausted-looking and very thin Roman, sitting on a milestone. He told them his name was Firstclasspostus and that he was one of Caesar's messengers. 'I'm responsible for carrying despatches between Britain and Rome,' he moaned between pants. 'But I'm not as young as I used to be and all this running is wearing me out!' Asterix pretended to be sympathetic, saying that they were going to Rome themselves and they would happily take any scrolls for him. Too tired to be suspicious, the messenger gratefully handed them his despatch-bag. As soon as they had turned the corner, though, the Gauls started to turn the bag inside out. 'Really, what a disgrace,' Asterix commented as they opened a secret password scroll. 'Some of these documents are dated three or four days ago!'

If OBELIX doesn't already carry it, put the PASSWORD SCROLL into his WAIST-SLIT. Now go to 111.

Since Obelix didn't have a translator, they still didn't have a clue what the Roman at the barrier was saying. He then suddenly started speaking in Gaulish, however, telling them that they were at the frontier with Helvetia (the Roman name for Switzerland). 'All right, all right, we understand you now!' Asterix exclaimed as the Roman began to repeat the information in Hispanic. But then he went on to say it in every other language he knew . . . and Asterix was becoming so fed up with him that he punched him on the nose. 'Oh no, I'd better take a magic potion!' he said as all the other Romans immediately drew their swords. When the last one had finally been sent through the air, the Gauls nonchalantly slipped under the barrier. 'Well, that's the language barrier dealt with!' Asterix chuckled as they walked into Helvetia.

*Remove a **MAGIC POTION CARD** from **ASTERIX'S WAIST-SLIT**. Now go to 135.*

Reaching the gangplank ahead of the other two, Asterix asked the ferryman to wait just a few seconds more. 'I hope little Dogmatix doesn't get seasick,' Obelix remarked with concern when they were all finally aboard. But, as they stepped off again at the other side of the lake, it was Obelix who looked the most green! 'We'd better look for somewhere where you can have something to eat,' said Asterix and they eventually found a small inn. When the waiter described what dishes they served, however, it was in a language the Gauls didn't understand. 'It sounds as if he can only speak Helvetian-Latin!' Asterix remarked and he asked his friend if he had a translator with him.

If OBELIX does have a TRANSLATOR, use it to find out what the waiter is saying by translating the content of his speech-balloon below. If he doesn't, go to 275 instead.

SUT LIM TIMA HOS TUL CHA PEX

213

'Okay, no uniforms!' the innkeeper told them when the Gauls said that they didn't have sixteen coins and, as soon as the Romans were at the door, he gave them away. 'What a sneak!' Asterix exclaimed as he quickly drank one of his magic potions. There were far too many Romans on this occasion for Asterix to knock *all* of them out but he was able to deal with enough to allow them to make a break for it. 'It seems such a shame to have to leave so many Romans standing!' Obelix remarked sadly when they had got safely away.

Remove a MAGIC POTION CARD from ASTERIX'S WAIST-SLIT. Now go to 77.

The three friends had just hidden themselves in the Patavium cart when they suddenly heard an ominous creaking sound from below. A moment later they were all lying flat on their backs in the street! 'You're obviously too heavy for it,' Asterix told his over-sized companion accusingly. 'We'll just have to try one of the other carts!' So they decided on the one for Luca this time, Obelix stepping in much more carefully. Fortunately, this cart was just about sturdy enough but, as it set off along the road, Asterix noticed that one of his magic potion gourds had burst. It must have happened in that tumble!

Remove a MAGIC POTION CARD from ASTERIX'S WAIST-SLIT. Now go to 52.

215

'I'm not sure this is the road we should have taken after all,' said Asterix, when they were about halfway to Juliobona. 'I can feel it in my bones!' At the mention of bones, Dogmatix suddenly became all excited but Asterix ordered him to keep quiet for a moment while he thought of how he could check that this was the right direction. Suddenly he spotted some Romans coming towards them and this gave him an idea. 'Hello,' he said to their leader, 'I think that Caesar of yours is a bit of a numbskull!' The soldiers immediately arrested them, saying that they were going to take them to Rome so they could repeat the remark to Caesar himself. As soon as they had found out which was the route to Rome, however, Asterix secretly drank one of his magic potions. 'Thanks very much for directing us!' he chuckled as he sent all their captors flying into the ditch.

Remove a MAGIC POTION CARD from ASTERIX'S WAIST-SLIT. Now go to 16.

216

Since they didn't have a translator, Asterix said they would just have to hope the guards *were* letting them through. So, they casually started to walk past but they'd only gone a couple of steps before the guards drew their swords on them. 'Perhaps they weren't telling us to go through after all!' Asterix remarked as he started to uncork one of his magic potions. A few clonks and thuds later, though, and the guards probably wished they had. For they were now all lying on the ground with stars before their eyes!

Remove a MAGIC POTION CARD from ASTERIX'S WAIST-SLIT. Now go to 34.

217

Obelix was the first to order, politely asking for a barrel of mead. 'A barrel!' the innkeeper exclaimed, not sure he had heard him correctly. 'Yes, please,' said Obelix. 'I only want a small amount because drink always goes straight to my head!' While they were talking over their drinks, a rather shifty-looking peasant came and sat at their table. 'Psst,' he whispered suddenly, 'I heard you mention an old Druid who was kidnapped by the Romans. For a price, I can give you some information about him.' Asterix asked what that price was and the peasant told him eleven coins – no more, no less!

Does OBELIX carry a COINBAG with him? If so, 'count out' the eleven coins by rotating the disc – then go to the number that appears on the other side. If not, go to 3 instead.

218
Choosing the cart for Gennes, the Gauls sat on the hay inside while they waited for the driver to come. 'Oh, I wonder what's keeping him?' Asterix tutted restlessly when the sundial on the wall showed that the driver was nearly a quarter of an hour late. 'You can never trust these carts to start on time!' At that moment, the cart for Vellaunodunum started to pull out and so the Gauls decided to take that one instead. As it happened, it was a good job they did because the Vellaunodunum driver told them that Gennes was completely in the opposite direction to Rome! **Go to 154.**

219
Asterix reached the galley first, asking the crew to wait just a few seconds more for his friends. When they were all aboard, the galley cast off and moved gracefully up the coast. 'Ah, this is the way to

travel!' Asterix remarked appreciatively as they all reclined in their hammocks. They had just dozed off in the hot sun when the captain came and tapped Asterix politely on the shoulder. 'Your fare will be nineteen coins,' he told him, 'but that does include use of all the facilities on the galley-deck; indoor and outdoor javelin-throwing, bathing tub, evening entertainment, etc!' Asterix nudged Obelix out of his sleep, asking if he had a coinbag with him.

If OBELIX does have a COINBAG, use it to 'count out' the nineteen coins by rotating the disc – then go to the number that appears on the other side. If he doesn't have one, go to 252 instead.

220

The Gauls spent their first night in Italia at a small country inn. For supper, they ordered three roast boar, lightly done, but the innkeeper looked as if he had never heard of such a dish. Instead, he brought them some strange flat things made of dough – and topped with olives and little fish. 'You no like my pizzas?' the innkeeper asked as the Gauls wondered how you were to eat them, and he looked so close to losing his temper that they thought they'd better take a bite. 'Right, who's going to try them first?' Asterix asked . . .

Throw the special DICE to decide which of the friends it's to be.

If you throw ASTERIX	go to 253
If you throw OBELIX	go to 93
If you throw DOGMATIX	go to 177

The Romans soon appeared – masses and masses of them! This time the odds were too great even for Asterix and Obelix and they decided just to surrender, hoping they would at least be put in the same cell as Getafix that way. But, instead, they were escorted away from the dungeons and then put on a galley that was leaving from the nearest harbour. After several days of being chained up in the galley's prison, they were finally thrown overboard just off the coast. Swimming ashore, they found that they were back at their village in Northern Gaul! Although they were glad to be home, they were very distressed about Getafix. 'I'm afraid we've failed him,' Asterix told the chief sadly. 'By now, he'll be inside the lions!' The chief told them there was no need for despair, though, because he had just heard that the Romans had put off his execution until the following month. So that just gave Asterix and his two friends time to go on another mission!

To help Asterix have another attempt at rescuing Getafix, you must start the game again. Try choosing a different item for Obelix to set out with this time, to see if it gives you any more luck.

'Ah, it's the most comfortable bed I've had in days!' Asterix exclaimed luxuriously as his two friends jumped into their hammocks as well. They all slept like logs (or *twigs* in little Dogmatix's case!) and, when they woke again in the morning, the galley was entering Cosa harbour. After having a good breakfast in the town, they prepared to get on their way once more but they couldn't decide which of three roads to choose. One went to Falerii, one to Narnia and one to Arretium. Unless Obelix had a map, they would just have to take pot-luck!

If OBELIX does have a MAP, use it to find out which of the three towns below is the nearest to Rome – then follow the appropriate instruction. If he doesn't have one, you'll have to guess which instruction to follow.

If you think it's FALERII	go to 170
If you think it's NARNIA	go to 248
If you think it's ARRETIUM	go to 95

223

'We'll just tell the guards that we're new servants for the palace,' Asterix told his friends as he led the way up to the huge stone gateway. The guards didn't believe them, though, saying that they looked more like assassins! 'If you're servants, why are you carrying that sword with you?' they asked. Having a quick think, Asterix replied that they were being employed as Caesar's bodyguards but the guards still didn't believe them, insisting that they give the palace password. 'And if you get it wrong,' they warned, 'you'll be thrown to the lions!'

Does OBELIX have a PASSWORD SCROLL with him? If so,

use it to find out the correct password by placing exactly over the scroll shape below – then follow the appropriate instruction. If he doesn't, you'll have to guess which instruction to follow.

```
P T TW   NN    I   R  H
 SA     I  J G T  N 8 O!

Q Q I N U    U B        R

M F  L S G         H C

   W U   B T T I U     A

 N ! N S         U  E 6

   K R B L O M

 W X I O T        S B 2

  A E C UC  U        S E

 U N N S      A S E

A   E  E  6 Q M M
```

If you think it's AUGUSTUS	go to 115
If you think it's JULIUS	go to 241
If you think it's TIBERIUS	go to 200

224

'*NEPTUNE* is correct,' said the centurion grudgingly, '– you may enter!' The Gauls were just slipping quietly past him when the centurion suddenly noticed little Dogmatix at their heels. 'Hey, wait a minute!' he called. 'How do I know that that dog of yours knows the password as well? My instructions are that *everyone* is to say it!' Obelix irritably brought Dogmatix back, making him give a couple of woofs for the centurion. 'There you are, that's "doggy" for *NEPTUNE*,' he told him, '. . . now are you satisfied?' Obelix's face was so red with annoyance that the centurion decided not to argue! ***Go to 72.***

Not long after Asterix started snoring, his two friends did so too – all dreaming of their favourite subjects. For Asterix, it was a Gaul completely free of Romans; for Obelix, it was a Gaul *full* of Romans so he could fight them all; and for Dogmatix it was a big dish of boar bones! It seemed no time at all before it was morning again but when Asterix and Obelix tried to stretch out their arms they found that someone had chained them behind their backs in the night! At that moment, a group of Romans appeared from behind a tree, gabbling in Latin to them. It would need a translator to work out what they were on about!

Does OBELIX carry a TRANSLATOR with him? If so, use it to work out what the Romans were saying by translating the instruction in the speech-balloon below. If not, go to 126 instead.

'My apologies, friends!' the waiter told them as soon as Obelix had given *DAGGER* as the password, and he shook the two Gauls warmly by the hand (and Dogmatix by the paw!). After he had served them the best boar he had, he asked them why they were so far from home. Licking the delicious boar sauce from his fingers, Asterix explained that they were going down to Rome to try and rescue a friend. 'In that case, you'll need a map of the Empire!' the waiter told them and he went into the back to fetch them one.

If OBELIX doesn't already carry it, put the MAP into his WAIST-SLIT. Now go to 67.

Dogmatix started yapping away as soon as he had opened his eyes, trying to make the other two wake up as well. After Asterix had trimmed his moustache and Obelix braided his pigtails, they all went down for breakfast. Obelix was hoping for some rashers of Danish boar but they were served a bowl of cereal and nuts instead. 'We call it muesli,' the chalet-owner told them. 'It's very healthy for you!' Obelix was in the middle of trying to convince him that boar could be very healthy for you as well – especially if you had to run after it yourself – when a patrol of Romans burst through the door. Their leader made some sort of declaration in Latin and Asterix asked his friend if he had a translator so they could work out what he was saying.

If OBELIX does have a TRANSLATOR, use it to find out what

the Roman's announcement was by translating the content of his speech-balloon below. If he doesn't, go to 190 instead.

SUT LIM TIMA HOS
TUL VOD TRO

'It looks as if *TIBERIUS* is wrong,' Obelix whispered to his friend as all the Romans started laughing. When the soldiers had finally stopped laughing, they ordered them to turn back but Obelix asked if he could have another guess at the password. This only made them start laughing again and Asterix drank one of his magic potions ready for the fight he could see coming. It was only a few minutes later that the Romans were all sprawled across the ground, the Gauls stepping coolly over the frontier. 'I wonder why they've suddenly stopped laughing?' Obelix asked with a satisfied grin on his face.

Remove a MAGIC POTION CARD from ASTERIX'S WAIST-SLIT. Now go to 220. (Remember: when there are no magic potion cards left in Asterix's waist-slit their mission has to stop, and you must start the game again.)

229

Not having a translator, the Gauls decided just to ignore what the Roman was shouting, hoping his voice would be drowned by all the other shouts. The next minute, though, he had jumped down and knocked Asterix's helmet off his head. Seeing this as a deliberate provocation, the little Gaul drank one of his magic potions. Soon the fight that was going on in the stands was much more interesting than the one going on in the arena! 'I don't know why we bother . . .' the gladiators remarked to each other as Roman after Roman came flying down at them from above. It was only when the Gauls had left the circus that Asterix suddenly realised what the officer must have been trying to tell him. 'I think he just wanted me to remove my helmet so he could see,' he said with a little embarrassment at all the devastation he had left behind!

Remove a MAGIC POTION CARD from ASTERIX'S WAIST-SLIT. Now go to 104.

230

'Cobbler's!' Asterix suddenly remarked as Obelix was in the middle of telling him how many Romans he reckoned he had knocked out on this mission. 'It isn't cobblers,' Obelix replied angrily but Asterix said that he meant he had just spotted a cobbler's – at the end of the street! When they had entered the shop, the cobbler asked Asterix to sit down while he measured his feet. He then set to work at making the most comfortable pair of shoes the little Gaul had ever tried. 'We Romans are famous for our fine footwear,' the cobbler told him proudly. He then gave them the bad news, however – the shoes would cost them thirteen coins!

Does OBELIX have a COINBAG with him? If so, use it to 'count out' the thirteen coins by rotating the disc – then turn to the number that appears on the other side. If not, go to 260 instead.

231

'Okay – no bribe, no dog!' the guard told them huffily when the Gauls said that they didn't have any coins. Since Asterix and Obelix weren't prepared to leave Dogmatix behind, it looked as if the only way they were going to enter the palace grounds was by force! So Asterix quickly drank one of his magic potions before helping his friend knock all the guards out. 'Honestly, these Romans seem to get crazier by the minute,' Asterix remarked as they now approached the palace doors. 'There we are pretending to be decorators, with swords in our belts and helmets on our heads . . . and all they're worried about is our dog!'

Remove a MAGIC POTION CARD from ASTERIX'S WAIST-SLIT. Now go to 34.

232

Tearing through the rain, it was Dogmatix who reached the inn first. The other two arrived soon after, Obelix panting away as Asterix knocked on the door. The innkeeper gave them a warm welcome, his pretty daughter bringing a cauldron of steaming hot soup to their table. 'Mmm, just what I needed,' said Obelix, 'and it's my favourite – oxtail!' They had nearly finished the soup when Asterix noticed a Roman paper on their table, *The Ancient Times*. 'Hey, look, there's a carving of Getafix on the front!' he exclaimed. The report underneath was in Latin, however, and so he asked his friend if he had a translator with him.

If OBELIX does have a TRANSLATOR, use it to find out what the report said by translating the heading below – then follow the instruction. If he doesn't, go to 263 instead.

Slowly reading his translator, Obelix announced that the Roman was telling them that they were at the frontier with Helvetia (the ancient name for Switzerland). '. . . and he's saying we can only cross into Helvetia,' Obelix continued, 'if we show him our passports.' Not possessing passports, Asterix was thinking they had no alternative but to force their way past but then he suddenly realised something, borrowing the translator for a moment. 'How *can* we show you a passport?' he demanded of the Romans. 'They haven't been invented yet!' While the Romans were reflecting on this slight oversight of theirs (standing there all these years waiting to check passports when there were no passports to check!), the Gauls nonchalantly slipped under the barrier. *Go to 135.*

234

Asterix crossed the frontier into Germania first, Obelix and Dogmatix following immediately behind. They eventually came to the town of Guntia and they looked round for an inn so they could have something to eat. Finding one, they were served with the traditional German fare of sausage and tankards of beer. 'Ooh, aren't the wild boar funny here,' Obelix remarked, picking up a sausage from his plate. 'Look, they're very tiny and skinny and have no legs!' After Obelix had finished off nearly every sausage in the inn, the Gauls decided it was time to be on their journey again. There were three roads leaving from Guntia – one for Argentoratum, one for Cambodunum and one for Divodurum – and Asterix said they should take the one that went in a southerly direction.

Does OBELIX carry a MAP with him? If so, use it to find out which of the three towns below is south from Guntia – then follow the appropriate instruction. If he doesn't, you'll have to guess which instruction to follow.

If you think it's ARGENTORATUM   go to 277
If you think it's CAMBODUNUM   go to 29
If you think it's DIVODURUM   go to 136

The Roman suddenly became very embarrassed, admitting that *EAGLE* was correct. He then tried to make it up to them, sitting between Asterix and Obelix and enthusiastically giving lots of information about his city. 'Of course, this circus isn't as big as the one in Rome,' he said proudly, putting an arm round each of them, 'but there's often just as much blood! And after you've seen the circus, why don't you visit our museum? Then there's the statue gallery . . .' In fact, he was so ashamed of the way he had treated these 'tourists' that he even offered them a bag of coins to pay for all their sight-seeing!

If OBELIX doesn't already carry it, put the COINBAG into his WAIST-SLIT. Now go to 104.

236

'Well done, Dogmatix,' said Asterix as the tiny mongrel suddenly started barking at a B and B sign pasted to the wall of a large hut. As he gave a knock on the door, Asterix confessed that B and B only stood for Bed and Breakfast – not boar or bone. 'But there's no need for you to get a "B" in your bonnet,' he chuckled as the door opened. They were met by a very friendly-looking, woman but when she began to speak they couldn't understand a word she was saying. Unless they had a translator with them, it looked as if they were going to have to try elsewhere!

Does OBELIX carry a TRANSLATOR? If so, use it to find out

what the woman is saying by translating her speech-balloon below – then follow the instruction. If not, go to 22 instead.

Some time later they found themselves back at the frontier with Gaul and so they realised Augustodunum must have been the wrong way. They had just started to turn back for one of the other routes, however, when the Romans guarding the border ordered them to stop. 'They must know that it was us who knocked out those sentries at the other frontier post,' Asterix said, hurriedly drinking one of his magic potions. But minutes later these sentries were all knocked out too, and the Gauls thought they had better get moving before they caused any more 'border incidents'!

Remove a *MAGIC POTION CARD* from *ASTERIX'S WAIST-SLIT*. Now go to 135.

Obelix boarded the galley first, the water coming another half-metre up the ship's sides as he did so! When Asterix and Dogmatix were also on board, the crew cast off and they were soon sailing gracefully up the coast towards Italia. 'As long as the wind doesn't drop, we should be there in a few hours,' Asterix said as they all reclined against some crates of export wine. Only about half an hour had passed, however, when they were forced to drop sail by a Roman galley blocking their course. The Romans jumped on board, interrogating all the crew to make sure none of them were spies heading for Italia. 'Hey, you there,' they bawled, suddenly noticing the Gauls. 'You don't look like crew members. Give us the correct password for a merchant galley in these waters!'

Does OBELIX carry a PASSWORD SCROLL with him? If so, use it to find out the correct password by placing exactly over the scroll shape below – then follow the appropriate instruction. If he doesn't, you'll have to guess which instruction to follow.

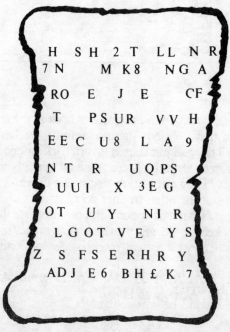

If you think it's JUPITER   go to 267
If you think it's MERCURY   go to 198
If you think it's NEPTUNE   go to 75

239

'Ah, this is much better than walking!' Asterix said contentedly as the cart they were hiding in rumbled towards Luca. 'Besides, it would be a pity to get dirty again after we'd just had that nice bath!' Obelix started to examine one of the togas they were lying on, asking his friend what they were for. When he found out that the long sheets of material were for wearing, he just couldn't believe it. 'I always said those Romans were crazy,' he exclaimed. 'Look, there aren't even any holes for their arms!' **Go to 52.**

240

'I expect they were taking Getafix to Vellaunodunum because it was a good place to lock him up for the night,' Asterix told his friend as the innkeeper finally went to fetch their order. 'They must have made their journey to Rome via the towns with the best prisons!' The innkeeper now returned with their drinks, laying them on the table. As he did so, he secretly slipped Asterix a roll of parchment from under his apron. 'If you're travelling all the way to Rome to rescue your friend,' he whispered, 'you'll need this list of passwords!'

If OBELIX doesn't already carry it, put the PASSWORD SCROLL into his WAIST-SLIT. Now go to 66.

241

'I knew you weren't really servants!' one of the guards exclaimed proudly after telling them that *JULIUS* was wrong. Seeing that they were about to be arrested, Asterix quickly drank one of his magic potions. 'Try not to make any more noise than you have to,' Asterix warned his friend as the two Gauls started thumping the Romans. 'We don't want to alert the rest of the palace guard!' When all the Romans at the gate had quietly been knocked out, the Gauls approached the palace doors. 'We'd better hurry before those guards come round again,' Asterix said as they entered.

Remove a *MAGIC POTION CARD* from *ASTERIX'S WAIST-SLIT*. Now go to 34.

242

'Woof, woof!' barked Dogmatix excitedly when *he* had picked the shortest straw. He immediately ran up to the sentry at the gate, giving him an affectionate lick on his ankles. Then he turned over on his back, demanding that the sentry tickle his tummy. 'How clever he is!' Obelix remarked proudly when his dog had the sentry completely distracted. Just as he and Asterix were slipping past, however, Obelix absent-mindedly asked the sentry whether *he* thought Dogmatix was a clever dog as well! The Roman suddenly threatened them with his pike, shouting something in Latin. Asterix quickly asked Obelix if he had a translator so they could work out what the sentry was saying and try and talk themselves out of this mess.

If *OBELIX* does have a *TRANSLATOR*, use it to translate the

content of the sentry's speech-balloon below – then follow the instruction to find out what he was saying. If he doesn't have one, go to 33 instead.

SUT LIM TIMA
HOS TUL VUR UMI

243

JAVELIN was obviously a bad guess, however, because the man suddenly slammed the door in their faces. 'But we *are* enemies of Rome,' the little Gaul shouted out, 'I'm the famous Asterix!' At this, the door slowly opened again and the man popped out his head. 'If you're Asterix,' he said, pointing across the muddy street, 'you should be able to lift that ox over there. I've heard that Asterix has superhuman strength!' Asterix happily obliged, raising the startled ox above his head with only one finger. Although the man now warmly invited them in, however, the feat had been so exhausting for Asterix that he had to have one of his magic potions.

Remove a MAGIC POTION CARD from ASTERIX'S WAIST-SLIT. Now go to 203.

Obelix had barely uttered *AUGUSTUS* as the password when the innkeeper hugged both him and Asterix to his chest, inviting them in as his welcome guests! Seeing all those Romans there made the Gauls feel quite uncomfortable and they said they would be happy to go straight off to bed for an early night. The Romans insisted that they join in some of their fun, however, and asked if they were any good at arm-wrestling. 'This is our unbeaten champion,' they said, pointing to one with a forearm as big as a tree trunk. 'Here's a bag of coins that says you won't be able to shift him!' So Obelix lazily lowered his elbow, instantly slamming the champion's arm against the table. 'Do you want to try the left one now?' he asked innocently as the Roman yelled for all he was worth.

If OBELIX doesn't already carry it, put the COINBAG into his WAIST-SLIT. Now go to 143.

Dogmatix just reached the inn door first, and he waited for the others to arrive so they could open it. The Gauls hadn't been sitting at a table long when a peculiar-looking man, dressed in an old wolf-skin, came and joined them. He said that he was a soothsayer and could read their future just by studying the boar bones on their plate. 'Perhaps you could tell us whether our mission to Rome will be successful, then?' Obelix asked naively. 'There's no point in going all that way if it won't!' he added. The soothsayer replied that his talent was a very rare one, however, and they would have to cross his palm with nine coins if he was to use it for them.

*Does **OBELIX** carry a **COINBAG** with him? If so, 'count out' the nine coins by rotating the disc – then go to the number that appears on the other side. If he doesn't have one, go to 185 instead.*

246
'He's saying that he's a tax-collector,' Obelix translated for his friend as the Roman repeated his announcement, '. . . and anyone who refuses to pay his taxes is to be thrown to the lions!' The Romans started moving round the breakfast tables, forcing everyone to give as much as they had. But, when they came to the Gauls' table, Obelix grabbed their leader by the throat, hurling him through the window. The others were soon following the same way and the Gauls calmly started their breakfast again. 'Yes, I think a few more nuts and this muesli could be very tasty!' Obelix remarked nonchalantly. *Go to 84.*

247
Following the road to Luca, Obelix asked his friend why the Romans were so fond of gladiator-fighting. 'It's because their pleasures are very uncivilised ones,' Asterix explained sadly. Obelix then asked if that's why all true Gauls were sworn to resist them. 'Partly,' Asterix replied, '. . . but also because we Gauls love a good scrap!' *Go to 104.*

They had gone several miles along the road to Narnia when they caught up with a cart of tomatoes being pulled by a horse. Discovering that the farmer in charge spoke Gaulish, Asterix thought it a good idea to check that they were heading the right direction. 'No, Rome be the other way,' the farmer replied. 'You should have taken the road for Falerii.' They were just about to turn back for the Falerii road when Asterix noticed how small the tomatoes in the cart were, hardly bigger than peas! The farmer said he just couldn't get them to grow properly and the little Gaul felt so sorry for him that he gave him one of his magic potions. 'A few drops of that on the plants,' he told him, 'and they'll be the size of water-melons!'

Remove a MAGIC POTION CARD from ASTERIX'S WAIST-SLIT. Now go to 149.

249

After having a bit of a think about it, the guard told them that *NEPTUNE* was incorrect and he would have to arrest them. 'But then you might give those purple spots to us,' said Asterix with his quick brain, 'and we could be indoors for weeks!' The guard immediately began to feel rather guilty about it, admitting how inconsiderate he had been. 'Well, never mind,' said Asterix, as he and his two friends strolled cheekily past him into the town, 'I'm sure you were only thinking of your duty!' ***Go to 14.***

The loud snoring sound rumbling through the wood proved that Obelix had gone to sleep first. In fact this awful noise wasn't much better than Cacofonix's singing and so the other two soon went to sleep as well to obliterate it! When it was morning again, Asterix suggested they try and buy breakfast on the journey, keeping their eyes open for an eating place along the roadside. 'Look, there's one!' cried Obelix, pointing to a little wooden hut with long-distance hay-carts parked around it. Their breakfast – crispy rashers of boar with wild mushrooms and fried bread – came to a total of fourteen coins, and Asterix asked his friend to open his coinbag so he could pay for it.

Does OBELIX have a COINBAG, though? If he does, 'count out' the fourteen coins by rotating the disc – then go to the number that appears on the other side. If he doesn't have one, go to 202 instead.

'*JUPITER* is correct – you may pass!' one of the Romans told them and the Gauls walked through into Helvetia. They had only gone a few steps more, however, when the Romans suddenly called them back, asking if they had anything to declare. Asterix and Dogmatix shook their heads but Obelix enthusiastically replied that he had. 'I'd like to declare that I'm very sad to be leaving my native Gaul,' he began, taking a long breath. 'And I'd like to declare that I've never much liked you Romans. And I'd like . . .' But before he could declare anything else, Asterix quickly dragged him away! **Go to 91.**

252
As soon as Asterix had told the captain that they didn't have any money with them, his manner completely changed. He said that they could choose between being thrown overboard or working the oars with the rest of the slaves below. Asterix decided on the oars, drinking one of his magic potions so that he would have enough strength. Even Dogmatix was made to earn his fare, having to give regular barks at the head of the oarsmen to make sure they all kept in time! 'It's not such a good way to travel now, is it?' Obelix remarked grumpily as the sweat poured off their backs.

Remove a MAGIC POTION CARD from ASTERIX'S WAIST-SLIT. Now go to 167.

253
'By Jupiter, they're not at all bad!' Asterix remarked as he decided to sample the pizzas first himself. 'In fact, a bit more melted goat's cheese on the top and they could be very tasty!' The innkeeper said

he would get them some more from the back but, as soon as he was out of sight, he told his wife to go and fetch some soldiers from the local garrison. 'Tell them that I think I've got some foreign spies in my inn,' he instructed her. 'They can't be Romans because they've never seen a pizza before!' It wasn't long before the soldiers were bursting in on the Gauls, demanding that they give the local password to prove that they were from this area.

Does OBELIX have a PASSWORD SCROLL with him? If so, use it to find out the correct password by placing exactly over the scroll shape below – then follow the appropriate instruction. If he doesn't, you'll have to guess which instruction to follow.

If you think it's LION	go to 168
If you think it's WOLF	go to 51
If you think it's EAGLE	go to 205

'No – *LION* is wrong!' the Roman barked when they'd made a guess at the password. 'Well, it's not completely wrong,' he added with a sinister chuckle, 'because that's what you're about to be thrown to!' He then ordered the Gauls to be taken down to the arena below. 'Oh, you get a much better view down here!' Obelix remarked delightedly to his friend as the lions started to circle them but Asterix was too busy drinking one of his magic potions. Then it was five minutes of the spectators' gasps and squeals of horror as the poor lions were sent reeling through the air. 'That was the most terrifying time of my life,' Obelix confessed when they were later walking round the streets again. 'I hated all those thousands of faces staring at me!'

Remove a *MAGIC POTION CARD* from *ASTERIX'S WAIST-SLIT*. Now go to 104.

They had only gone a short way along the road to Araines when half a dozen rough-looking men suddenly jumped out of the bushes in front of them. 'We're bandits,' they shouted. 'Give us everything you have!' Always eager to please, Obelix immediately started searching through his pockets but then the bandits added that, if they didn't pay up, they would have to fight. It was a rather silly thing to say because a fight was something Obelix could never resist! 'Okay, we give up, we give up!' they all whimpered after they had been given a good drubbing by him. They even started searching through their own pockets to see what *they* could give, one of them offering Obelix a password scroll.

If OBELIX doesn't already carry it, put the PASSWORD SCROLL into his WAIST-SLIT. Now go to 117.

256

Seeing that the Gauls didn't have twenty coins, the innkeeper immediately invited the Romans in. 'Here are two likely suspects!' he told them with a grin. But the grin soon disappeared as the Romans were sent spinning into every corner of the room. 'That's made me use up one of my precious magic potions,' Asterix told him angrily as the Gauls prepared to start on the innkeeper, but he begged them to leave him alone, saying that they could have as much food as they could eat. Asterix wasn't prepared to be bribed but Obelix held his friend back, starting to think of platter upon platter of roast boar. 'After all, two against one would be bullying a bit!' he told him.

Remove a MAGIC POTION CARD from ASTERIX'S WAIST-SLIT. Now go to 143.

257

Asterix reached the inn first, immediately entering and looking for a spare bench. As soon as he had found one, he called over the waiter so they could order. 'What's Boar à la King?' he asked, studying the menu and, since it sounded quite delicious, they decided to choose that. But at that moment everything in the inn went absolutely quiet. 'Boar à la King is a fake dish to test whether my customers are true Gauls or not,' the waiter told them accusingly. 'Since you were taken in by it, you must be Roman spies!' When Asterix protested their innocence, the waiter replied that he would only believe them if they were able to give the correct local password.

Does OBELIX carry a PASSWORD SCROLL with him? If so, use it to find out the correct password by placing exactly over the scroll shape below – then follow the appropriate instruction. If he doesn't have one, you'll have to guess which instruction to follow.

If you think it's SWORD   go to 194
If you think it's JAVELIN   go to 17
If you think it's DAGGER   go to 226

258

It was only a few more miles before they arrived at Octodurus and they went into one of the little wooden shops to buy some boar pies for their journey. The shopkeeper said they didn't sell much boar in Helvetia, though – their main diet being bars of a sweet brown stuff. 'We call it chocolate,' he told them, 'and it comes with all sorts of nuts and centres.' Obelix asked if he had any boar-centred ones but the shopkeeper said that the two flavours didn't go very well. 'I can't see your chocolate stuff ever catching on, then!' Obelix remarked huffily as they walked out of the shop. *Go to 91.*

259

The Romans told them that *LION* was correct and that they could step on to the rope-car. 'I hope this thing is safe,' said Asterix as the little wooden cabin wobbled uncertainly across the gorge. He knew the Romans were masters of engineering but he did sometimes wonder whether they tried to be a bit *too* advanced! Seeing they were foreigners, an old Helvetian travelling with them started to tell them about the many languages that were spoken in his country. In fact, he said it was so confusing that they really ought to have a translator. 'Here, take my spare!' he said kindly, producing one from his tunic.

If OBELIX doesn't already have it, put the TRANSLATOR into his WAIST-SLIT. Now go to 84.

'I'm afraid we don't have any coins with us,' Asterix told the cobbler regretfully. So he sadly handed the shoes back but then he suddenly had an idea. 'Why don't I pay you with one of my magic potions instead?' he suggested. 'A few drops of that every morning and you'll be able to make ten times as many shoes!' Sampling the potion, the cobbler agreed it was a fair swap and so let the Gauls take the shoes away. And from that moment on, he no longer had to *cut* the leather – he just tore it with his bare hands!

Remove a *MAGIC POTION CARD* from *ASTERIX'S WAIST-SLIT*. Now go to 79.

261

The Romans' leader told the Gauls that *SHIELD* was correct but asked why they didn't want to wear sandals like everyone else. 'Because I'm fed up with my toes getting wet in the rain,' Asterix replied, trying to think of something. 'Yes, and it rains a lot in Gaul!' Obelix added innocently but, fortunately, the last of the Romans had just left the shop. The cobbler felt so embarrassed at his mistrust that he not only made Asterix's shoes for free but he even gave them a coinbag with the day's profits!

If *OBELIX* doesn't already carry it, put the *COINBAG* into his *WAIST-SLIT*. Now go to 79.

262

It was Dogmatix who decided on his order first, lapping at the table to show that he would like some goat's milk. 'How do you know that means goat's milk?' the innkeeper asked as Obelix interpreted for him, but Obelix said it was easy – Dogmatix always had goat's milk! The innkeeper was just returning with their drinks when a patrol of Roman soldiers burst in, saying that they had heard reports of some rebels from outside being in town. 'Here you, you look unfamiliar,' the leader said, pointing to Obelix. 'I'll test you. What's the special password the town uses on Caesar's birthday?'

Does OBELIX carry a PASSWORD SCROLL? If so, use it to find out the correct password by placing exactly over the shape below – then follow the instruction. If he doesn't, you'll have to guess which instruction to follow.

```
P  MF  LAß  A      6P
M J      U6 A    S QN
   O TO        UL    K K
   L   66G  D I A R R
   7 R S B N  H  S H
     M E M E 2 U    U
   N S   L T  V L
   J AR  6   I FH 5F
     I  J U W T     R
   Q UQ  S      U W S O O
   T L R 7 N   H 8 O P I
```

If you think it's AUGUSTUS   go to 31
If you think it's JULIUS   go to 142
If you think it's TIBERIUS   go to 209

263

When Obelix said that he didn't have a translator, Asterix tried to think of some other way that they could find out what the report was about. He asked the innkeeper and his daughter whether either of them knew Latin but they regretfully replied that they didn't. 'There must be *some* way!' said Asterix, racking his brains. After quite a time, though, Obelix suddenly announced that he had an idea. 'I know,' he exclaimed, nearly causing Asterix and Dogmatix to stop breathing in their suspense, '. . . let's have some more of that delicious soup!' ***Go to 143.***

264

It was Asterix who opened his eyes first, being woken by a strange clock on the wall with a little wooden boar popping out. The boar grunted eight times to show that it was eight o'clock. 'These

Helvetians have some funny inventions,' Asterix said when his two friends were awake as well. 'Next, they'll be putting cuckoos into their clocks!' The Gauls now left the chalet, soon arriving at a deep gorge. Fortunately, there was a rope-car (the ancient equivalent of a cable-car) across the gorge but it was operated by Romans and they would only let them on if they knew the right password!

Does OBELIX have a PASSWORD SCROLL with him? If so, use it to find out the correct password by placing exactly over the scroll shape below – then follow the appropriate instruction. If Obelix doesn't have one, you'll have to guess which instruction to follow.

```
A7  OE    F  Aß   B A8 M
D E      8W S      U Z
  WN   O      TA    M L
  Z L  ET G   NU N
    W L  S DR U  2 O
  F     F I W T    P
  S L   A N N A S
   F  I  H O 4 I R
 N S E    R        R
 A O T B    IB N G
 T F U B R   E 4 U
```

If you think it's LION	go to 259
If you think it's WOLF	go to 6
If you think it's EAGLE	go to 166

'First, there is cider fondue – which is melted cheese laced with cider,' Obelix translated as the waiter started to list the dishes again. 'Then, there is wine fondue – which is melted cheese laced with wine,' he said. 'Then there is beer fondue – which is melted cheese laced with beer. Then there is mead fondue . . .' In fact, all the dishes seemed to consist of melted cheese – not a nice piece of roast boar amongst them! 'These Helvetians must be very fond of their fondue,' Obelix remarked moodily as they tried to decide which to choose. *Go to 20.*

'Our apologies,' the Goths told them after admitting that *JAVE-LIN* was the correct password, 'you're not spies after all! But how is it that you don't know our cake?' Asterix replied that they were from the top corner of Gaul and had never been to this part of Germania before. The Goths therefore offered them a map, saying that it was very easy to get lost in the big forest.

If OBELIX doesn't already have it, put the MAP into his WAIST-SLIT. Now go to 157.

'So you *are* crew-members, then!' the leader of the Romans said grudgingly when *JUPITER* proved correct. 'But what about this little dog here – surely he isn't a crew-member as well?' Asterix quickly put his brain into action, saying that Dogmatix was the ship's mascot. 'Then why is it that he looks so seasick?' the Roman asked, remaining suspicious. Obelix thought it was time to put his brain into action as well. 'How could a dog that size have drunk the whole of the sea?' he demanded, '. . . and if he had, of course it would make him sick!' The Romans were so confused by this answer that they returned to their galley! *Go to 167.*

268

After Dogmatix had settled in his little hammock, the two Gauls jumped into theirs as well. Unfortunately, though, it was a very calm night and so the slaves had to be used in the rowing deck below to power the galley. 'I hardly slept a wink,' Asterix complained the following morning. 'You'd think the slave-master would crack his whip a little more quietly at night-time!' The galley was now entering Cosa harbour but, just as our heroes stepped ashore, they were arrested by Roman soldiers. 'You three look like Gaulish spies,' their leader told them. 'If you can't tell us the town password we'll know that you are!'

Does OBELIX carry a PASSWORD SCROLL with him? If so, use it to find out the correct password by placing exactly over the

scroll shape below – then follow the appropriate instruction. If he doesn't, you'll have to guess which instruction to follow.

```
7 O GG O NN8U T
M 2    E SN    O 3 M E
   V H V U    H    R Z 7
  S E  9PS I      A O N
  C 3 L    R LSL C
  D RS   LTS      M
    O    D V A A V
  V M J V   CU D
  N O T E 8 9      T
  Y  EEYR    N T N
   L O   LOH 3 H
```

If you think it's **SHIELD**	go to 10
If you think it's **HELMET**	go to 131
If you think it's **ARMOUR**	go to 206

Not having a translator, the Gauls just continued to examine the sandals. When the Romans touched Asterix again, however, it wasn't a tap this time but a heavy clout on the head! 'Right, that's it!' the little Gaul said furiously and he quickly drank one of his magic potions. A few minutes later, it was only the fat youngster who was left standing . . . and he was excitedly jumping up and down at all the action. 'What a bloodthirsty people these Romans are,' Asterix remarked disapprovingly. 'Look, even their young children seem to be that way!'

Remove a MAGIC POTION CARD from ASTERIX'S WAIST-SLIT. Now go to 79.

270

There were still another fifty milestones to go to Araines when they spotted a fairly large town just across the valley. Since this one was obviously a good deal closer, they decided to change their direction for that. A sign was soon welcoming them to the town of Aregenua and Asterix was relieved to see that the gates were unguarded. 'I suppose you're a little disappointed, though?' he asked his friend sarcastically as they passed through. Obelix realised it would be a bit unwise to nod his head! *Go to 81.*

'*MERCURY* is correct,' the guard said, letting the Gauls pass, '– and thank you for telling me about my purple spots!' Now that they were inside the town, the three travellers made straight for an inn so they could get something to eat. Over their delicious meal of wild boar and French fries (or Gaulish fries as they were called then!), they discussed the long journey ahead of them. 'If you're going all the way to Rome,' said a beggar at their side, listening in on their conversation, 'you'll encounter many languages. For a slice of that delicious boar there, I'll give you a translator to help you!'

If OBELIX doesn't already carry it, put the TRANSLATOR into his WAIST-SLIT. Now go to 14.

'I'll have a tankard of mead please,' Asterix told the innkeeper while the other two were still deciding. Since his friends were taking so long about it, he then asked the innkeeper if he had seen the Romans bring an old Druid through that way. 'Yes, I did,' the innkeeper replied. 'A peculiar old man – with a long white beard and three strands of hair sticking out of his head! I heard the Romans say that they were taking him to a town just south of Lutetia for the night.' Asterix told Obelix to forget about his order for a moment and check whether he had a map tucked in his breeches so they could see what this town was called.

Does OBELIX have a MAP with him? If so, use it to find out which of the three towns below is south from Lutetia – then follow the appropriate instruction. If he doesn't, you'll have to guess which instruction to follow.

If you think it's AREGENUA	go to 15
If you think it's VELLAUNODUNUM	go to 240
If you think it's CAESAROMAGUS	go to 174

273

'No, *JULIUS* is wrong!' said the innkeeper and he instantly slammed the door in Asterix's face. Asterix was mad enough at this rudeness as it was but when a cold drop of rain fell down his neck he became absolutely incensed! Quickly drinking a magic potion, he smashed the door down and strolled right into the midst of the Romans. By the time Obelix and Dogmatix had arrived, there were stunned bodies everywhere. 'Now perhaps you could show us to our room,' Asterix said to the trembling innkeeper, '– and I wouldn't mind a little hot goat's milk being delivered for my nightcap!'

Remove a *MAGIC POTION CARD* from *ASTERIX'S WAIST-SLIT*. Now go to 143.

'You've got the password wrong!' one of the Romans replied when the Gauls made a guess at *MERCURY*. 'You're not allowed to cross!' Of course, the Gauls had other ideas. Asterix quickly drank one of his magic potions. 'Now, are you going to let us pass or not?' he demanded, giving the sentries one last chance. The Romans started laughing at the audacity of this little man but, a few minutes later, they were all sprawled across the ground! 'Oh, we forgot to ask if you had anything to declare . . .' one of the battered soldiers called after them wearily as the Gauls stepped across the frontier, but his mates quickly told him to shut up!

Remove a *MAGIC POTION CARD* from *ASTERIX'S WAIST-SLIT*. Now go to 91.

Since Obelix didn't have a translator, they just indicated to the waiter to bring *any* dish. Ten minutes later, he was carrying a large cauldron of melted cheese to their table with little pieces of bread. The Gauls didn't realise that they were meant to dip the bread into the cheese, however, and just drank it straight from the cauldron in huge gulps. It wasn't long before they all had bad tummy-aches, barely able to walk into the open air again. 'I feel as if all my strength has gone,' Asterix remarked weakly, his feet dragging along the ground. 'I'd better have one of my magic potions in case we meet any Romans!'

Remove a *MAGIC POTION CARD* from *ASTERIX'S WAIST-SLIT*. Now go to 20.

276

'There's a cobbler's!' Obelix exclaimed, suddenly spotting a shop with animal hides hanging from it just across the square. Entering the shop, Asterix asked the cobbler to make him a new pair of shoes, adding that he was a size seven. The cobbler suddenly screamed for assistance, though, and it was only a matter of seconds before the shop was full of Roman soldiers. 'These people must be spies from another country,' he told their leader. 'They ordered shoes instead of our customary sandals!' The Roman's leader agreed that it was pretty strong evidence against them but said he would give them the benefit of the doubt if they could tell him the town password.

Does *OBELIX* have a *PASSWORD SCROLL* with him? If so, use it to find out the correct password by placing exactly over the

scroll shape below – then follow the appropriate instruction. If he doesn't, you'll have to guess which instruction to follow.

If you think it's SHIELD	go to 261
If you think it's HELMET	go to 11
If you think it's ARMOUR	go to 138

'No, this can't be right,' Asterix said when they had been following the Argentoratum road for quite a few miles. 'Look, we've come back to the border with Gaul again!' So they returned to Guntia, deciding on the road for Cambodunum this time. On the way, they saw some Goths doing a dance where they slapped each other's legs and faces. Unfortunately, however, Obelix didn't realise it was a dance, and thinking there was a fight going on he rushed in to see if he could help. Seconds later, there *was* a fight going on – with Obelix against all thirty or forty dancers! Asterix quickly drank one of his magic potions before going to his friend's assistance. 'All they were doing was having a bit of fun!' the little Gaul told Obelix crossly when they had knocked out all the Goths.

Remove a MAGIC POTION CARD from ASTERIX'S WAIST-SLIT. Now go to 157.

278

Scanning his translator, Obelix told Asterix that the sentry was shouting to them to stay where they were. 'He's now saying that he knows what we're up to,' Obelix added, 'and that he won't be made a monkey of!' But Dogmatix turned over on his back again and the Roman couldn't resist giving him another tickle. He soon wished that he hadn't, though, because Dogmatix suddenly snapped at his fingers, making him run off in pain! 'It's a good job your dog's rather cleverer than you are!' Asterix told Obelix as they all now calmly entered the town. **Go to 81.**

A sort of doggy snoring noise told the other two that Dogmatix was now in the land of dreams and it wasn't long before they were in that land too. It seemed no time at all before it was morning again and they all had a good stretch, ready to continue on their journey. They had just passed the large town of Lutetia when they reached a signpost pointing three ways. One arm pointed to Caesaromagus, one to Juliobona and the other to Vellaunodunum. Asterix asked his friend if he had a map with him so they would know which road they should take for the south.

If OBELIX does have a MAP, use it to find out which of the towns is south of Lutetia – then follow the instruction. If he doesn't have one, you'll have to guess which instruction to follow.

If you think it's CAESAROMAGUS   go to 109
If you think it's JULIOBONA   go to 215
If you think it's VELLAUNODUNUM   go to 32

'Blacklegs!' the striking slaves all shouted down at them as Asterix was the first to swim to the other side of the river. The little Gaul was about to shout some abuse back but, when he glanced down, he noticed that he *did* have black legs – that river must have been filthy! Fortunately, they soon reached the spa town of Augustodunum and they were able to give themselves a good wash at the public baths. 'I wonder which way now?' Asterix asked as, just on leaving Augustodunum, they came to a signpost which pointed three directions. One arm was for Valentia, another for Avaricum and the third for Tolosa.

Does OBELIX have a MAP with him? If so, use it to find out which of the three towns is in the right direction for Rome from Augustodunum – then follow the appropriate instruction. If he doesn't have a map, you'll have to guess which instruction to follow.

If you think it's VALENTIA   go to 210
If you think it's AVARICUM   go to 165
If you think it's TOLOSA   go to 83

281

They eventually realised that the branch for Vesontio wasn't the one they wanted, though, because it brought them back to the frontier with Gaul. Dogmatix gave a little whine on seeing his own country again and Obelix couldn't help the odd tear as well. As they were forced to turn back for one of the other branches, Asterix was wondering what he could do to cheer his companions up but then he suddenly spotted a patrol of Romans ahead. Of course – what better?! He quickly gave Dogmatix one of his magic potions and then leant against a tree while his two friends spent five minutes terrorising the poor patrol. 'I feel a lot better now!' Obelix said with a smile as they continued on their way.

Remove a *MAGIC POTION CARD* from *ASTERIX'S WAIST-SLIT*. Now go to 135.

282

They hadn't been on the Brigantium road for long when they came across a signpost pointing to Noricum (the Roman name for Austria). 'Oh no, that means we must be heading east!' exclaimed Asterix and he said they would have to turn back for one of the other roads. Deciding on the road for Bergomum this time, they were soon high up in the mountains and Asterix and Dogmatix started to shiver from the cold. 'Personally, it's not the cold I mind,' commented Obelix. 'It's that there doesn't seem to be any wild boar to catch up here.' He added that he had noticed the odd mountain goat or two but they never seemed to have quite the same flavour! *Go to 20.*

Since they weren't able to pay, the slave summoned the owner of the baths, who told them that they would have to massage fifty Romans each before they could leave. 'And I want it done properly,' he insisted. 'Every single little muscle or I'll have you arrested!' Asterix drank one of his magic potions in preparation for this strenuous task but Obelix couldn't wait to get started, going from one sleeping Roman to the next. 'Please, please, ask him to stop,' they all begged the owner as Obelix delightedly thumped and pounded their backs. 'He's breaking every bone we've got!' As the Gauls were forced to leave, Asterix complained that he had used up one of his magic potions for nothing. But Obelix wasn't really listening, thinking that massaging was almost as much fun as fighting!

*Remove a **MAGIC POTION CARD** from **ASTERIX'S WAIST-SLIT**. Now go to 52.*

They hadn't followed the Patavium road far when they caught up with a large group of slaves being coaxed along with whips. Asterix asked one of them if they were on their way to Rome but he said they were going to a place called Venice, to try and stop it falling into the water! 'For Rome, you'd better take the next right turn,' he added as the whip came down on his back again. 'Look, there's one ahead!' To show his gratitude, Asterix secretly gave the slave one of his magic potions, whispering to him that if he and his friends all took a drop each they would be ten times as powerful. 'Thanks,' the slave replied appreciatively, rather misunderstanding Asterix's meaning. 'Now we'll be able to work ten times as hard!'

Remove a MAGIC POTION CARD from ASTERIX'S WAIST-SLIT. Now go to 104.